IT'S AN UNDEAD THING

Zooey Zombie #1

Check out Alex Apostol's other zombie novels available on Amazon, Kindle eBooks, and Audible.

Dead Soil (Dead Soil #1)
Dead Beginnings Volume 1
Dead Beginnings Volume 2

And Alex Apostol's other novels
Broken Angel
(Chronicles of a Supernatural Huntsman #1)
Earth Angel
(Chronicles of a Supernatural Huntsman #2)
Hunted Angel
(Chronicles of a Supernatural Huntsman #3)
Girls Like Us: A Novel

And her non-fiction journals
Novel Notes: A Guided Writing Journal
Novel Notes: Series Edition

CHAPTER ONE

Three men in navy blue jumpsuits walked the Boston Common with animal control poles. The loops at the ends swayed with each cautious step they took, careful not to make a sound as they stalked through the trees. Everything was quiet. Even the birds held their breaths, not letting a single peep fall from their beaks. Every so often, a gentle summer breeze rustled through the branches, making the three men turn on their heels.

"Didn't we clear this area two days ago?" the youngest man in the back whispered.

He was twenty-five-years-old and the newest member of the National Guard's zombie division, a special unit meant to catch and cure walking corpses. A rush of adrenaline made the young man's hands shake every time they were dispatched. Three men was not enough for the task in his opinion, but ever since the plague took a good chunk of the population the military had been left short-handed.

"And now we're clearing it again," the man closest to him hissed through his teeth.

Sergeant Stone's name suited him as he was built like a solid wall of chimney. His lips were pursed so thinly, it was a wonder how they didn't disappear altogether. He was tired of the newbie always questioning everything. It was their job to shut up and follow orders. If they didn't, the zombies could very well take over again.

The reign hadn't lasted long thanks to all the zombie lore from comic books, movies, and television. The CDC had even implemented a plan for if the zombie plague ever broke out due to the popularity of the monsters. No one ever thought it would really happen, until it did. And then, the government was quick to act. Sergeant Stone was one of the first to volunteer for the division.

He laughed when the Major told him a nineteen-year-old was joining the team that morning. He wasn't laughing now that they were out in the field.

"Would you two shut your traps?" their commanding officer growled from the lead. "We're looking for flesh-eating, organ-chewing, blood-drinking zombies, or have you forgotten why we're here?"

He was a decorated war hero who served three tours in Afghanistan and one in Iraq. His hair was silver and thinning, and his arms sagged with muscles that had been ignored over the years. It was the pins on his breast-pocket alone that commanded respect.

"No, sir," they whispered in unison.

"Good, then come on."

Together they walked in a U-shape, Major Jackson facing forward and leading the way while the newbie, Private First Class Goodman, faced the East and Sergeant Stone faced the West. There should have been someone watching their six, but they were told they would have to do without for a while.

The rustle of shambling footsteps sounded ahead.

The Major held up a fist, stopping the other two in their tacks.

A dull groan echoed off the trees.

Major Jackson pointed to Sergeant Stone and motioned for him to circle around and come up from behind. The Sergeant moved with stealth, his feet not making a sound on the plush grass. Goodman felt his knees knock together as he lost sight of his comrade. There were only two of them now.

Up ahead, a female limped slowly out into the open from behind a tree.

"Ma'am!" The Major called out with his catcher's pole gripped in both hands.

He knew she wasn't going to respond, but protocols had to be followed, even if they were stupid.

The young woman opened her mouth and let out a hiss before clacking her teeth together.

The two men nodded once to each other and watched as the dirtied woman moved toward them, her arms raising up in front of her. Her long brown hair was matted with twigs, dirt, and dried blood. A good shower would detangle that mess. Her pale face was scratched, but not so badly that she wouldn't recover in time. The only substantial wound visible was the chunk that had been bitten from her trapezius, nothing that couldn't be cleaned, stitched together, and grafted over.

"Let's bring her in," the Major declared.

They advanced on the pitiful zombie.

"Z-729657," the Major said in an official tone, "you're coming with us to the Massachusetts General Hospital where you will be admitted into the Undead Ward for treatment and—AHHH!"

A large male had wandered up soundlessly from behind and sunk his teeth into the Major's arm. He munched relentlessly as screams pierced the air. His head was thrown around as the Major tried to shake his bloodied arm free.

Goodman stood frozen in horror. It was the first time he'd seen anyone attacked up close. Crimson spilled from the Major's arm onto the green grass. His Commanding Officer was losing his pallor before his eyes. Though his legs were unable to move, his stomach gave a violent lurch.

"What are you doing?! Catch it!" Sergeant Stone's gruff voice called as he ran up to them.

He didn't wait for Goodman to snap out of it, but secured the female zombie by the neck with his own catcher's pole. She struggled listlessly as he held her in place. Her growls echoed in the young Private's ears, debilitating him further. His vision tunneled and all he could see were her bloodied, gnashing teeth with bits of the Major's skin hanging from between.

"For fuck's sake," Sergeant Stone growled.

He shoved the catcher's pole with the secured zombie into the petrified kid's hands and snatched his away. With precision and ease, he slipped the loop around the male zombie's neck and yanked him away from the shrieking Major, taking a chunk of arm with him.

Major Jackson dropped to his knees, howling. The blood flowed from the gaping wound like a raging river. He tried to stop the bleeding with his hand, but his life-force gushed between his fingers. With his free hand, the Sergeant pulled the Major up by the collar.

"You'll be fine, Sir. They'll get you fixed up with some of that Zombutexa-whatever-the-fuck it's called, and you'll be good to go."

"I don't want to become one of them," the forty-eight-year-old man wept while clutching his arm.

The Sergeant rolled his eyes. "You're not going to turn into one of them. Now, come on. Let's get them in the van and get out of here before any more show up." He snatched the other pole from the frightened kid and led both zombies across the park.

The corpses bumped into each other, hissing and clawing at the air for freedom, while the Major whimpered from behind. They left the Private dumbstruck in the blood-stained grass.

"Let's go, fuck-shit, before we leave your ass here!"

Goodman snapped out of his horrified daze and jogged to catch up. He went to take one of the poles, but the Sergeant jerked it away. The two zombies stumbled sideways and let out a series of moans and growls.

"I don't think so, newbie. Not after what you just pulled."

"I didn't mean to—" the copper-haired, wiry kid started to say.

"Save it. It's not up to me what happens to you now."

When they reached the Army-green van, Sergeant Stone ushered the dead up the ramp and into the back. He released the loops from the poles with the press of a button. Sensing their freedom, the two bodies lunged forward. Stone slammed the doors and peered in through the tiny window. He smiled with all his crooked teeth.

"Not today, motherfuckers!"

The Major groaned loudly from the other side of the van, as if death himself were approaching to take him away.

"All right, all right," the Stone grumbled as he walked around to the driver's side. "Let's go."

Goodman hopped in first and held a hand out. The Major, refusing to take it or possibly not seeing it through his blinding pain, inched his way through the passenger door and onto the seat. The smell of copper immediately overwhelmed everyone onboard.

The van lurched forward and a loud thud came from the back. Stone gave a satisfied chuckle as he turned onto Tremont Street. The Major let out another dramatic groan as Goodman stared at his wound with a gaping mouth. The kid nudged closer to Stone without realizing it. The Sergeant nudged him with his elbow.

"You wanna sit in my lap, Goodman?"

"Sorry," he mumbled as he readjusted himself, and then he whispered, "do you think he's going to be okay?"

The Major had leaned his head against the cool glass of the window. His eyes slowly closed as he struggled to breathe properly. He looked like he'd aged ten years in the last ten minutes.

"He'll be fine. Takes a good twenty-four hours to zombify completely. They'll give him the shot and that will be that."

"That will be that," Goodman repeated as he nodded his head.

He had no choice but to believe his Sergeant. After all, the hardened man had been on countless zombie hunts since hospitals all over the country opened the Undead Wards at the beginning of the year. He'd been through three Commanding Officers and eight teams of men. No one had ever died on a mission, though a good number had been bitten, infected for life with the zombie plague. But Stone believed it was all part of the job. The military had never been a safe career. This plague didn't change that.

Goodman wondered if he stayed with the division if he would become callous like Sergeant Stone. The very thought sent a shiver down his spine. He tried to ignore the muffled groans and bangs from the back. No matter how many he came face-to-face with, he would never get used to the sight of a zombie hungry for his brains. When he decided to sign up for the division, all he thought about was the gratitude others would feel toward him for helping to make their city safe again. It wasn't until today that he realized there was so much more to the job, like the zombies. He thought most of them had been cured already. If they allowed him to, he resolved to do better on the next mission.

In the back, the two zombies tried to stay standing as the van took sharp turns. The female moaned each time her head hit the hard metal side, but she didn't feel any pain. She couldn't feel anything but the overwhelming desire to sink her teeth into warm, flesh to get to the gooey brains underneath. The other zombie had been so close to securing their meal. If only they hadn't been outnumbered, they would both be on cloud nine right now, riding a brain high for the rest of the day.

The mangled man she'd been picked up with looked at her. He parted his crusted lips as if he were going to speak, but all that came out was a deep groan. He continued to stare as the van rocked with each turn. His wobbly legs offered little help to keep him upright. With each fall, he turned away and grunted.

She'd seen this zombie before in the park. He was vicious and moved with an agility the rest had lost over time. When it came to brains, this guy wasn't messing around. He wanted them bad and he would attack anyone to get them. A part of her felt scared to be alone with him, but then she remembered—zombies don't eat other zombies. It's rule number one.

Chapter Two

Zooey Beckett opened her eyes. The repetitive beep of the electrocardiograph machine seemed to grow louder with each ounce of consciousness she gained. Her head felt like it'd been hit with a sledgehammer, her face and shoulders stung and ached, but she was alive! At least, she thought she was.

She went to move her hand to touch it lightly to her throbbing cheek, but was stopped midway. A loud metallic clank echoed in the empty room.

"What the—" she said in a raspy voice unlike her own.

Metal handcuffs chained both her hands to each side of a hospital bedrail. Panic rose in her chest like a fire. Her heartbeat raced, sending the machine into a frenzy. She thrashed herself about, trying to get loose.

"Somebody get me out of here!" she yelled, not sure if there was anyone around to hear her.

She vaguely remembered someone telling her they were taking her to the hospital, but she wasn't sure why. Her brain felt light and clouded over with fog.

"Help!" she cried out. "Please help!"

Finally, the door opened and a young male nurse in green scrubs with too much gel in his dark, straight hair strode in. He turned off the EKG and shoved a thermometer in her ear.

"Hold still," he said dryly.

Every breath was shallow and painful, and she was still confused. She ignored the nurse's demands and moved about as much as her restraints would allow.

"Why am I here? What's going on? What did I do?"

Crusty-haired nurse ignored her and took the thermometer out when it beeped, though with as much as she moved the reading couldn't have been accurate. He wrote on his notepad and moved around to the other side of the bed, removing his stethoscope from around his thin neck.

"Can you tell me what happened?" she urged again. "Please!"

He placed the cold metal to her chest and looked up at the ceiling to avoid her desperate gaze.

Just then, a tall slender man in a white labcoat walked in.

"Hello, I'm Doctor Evan Fullerton. I will be your resident doctor for the duration of your stay."

Zooey's eyes grew wide as tears gathered in them. "What do you mean? Tell me why I'm here!" Blind rage was creeping up in her. She needed answers.

The doctor removed his silver-rimmed glasses and placed them in his breast pocket. The nurse rolled a chair in from the hallway and placed it behind the doctor, who lowered himself without ever taking his eyes off Zooey.

"What's the last thing you remember, Miss…?"

She looked from him to the nurse. Her mouth fell open in bewilderment. "Zooey Beckett," she said harshly.

"Ah," the doctor sighed while nodding his salt and peppered head. "Miss Beckett. As detailed as you can, please tell me the last thing you remember."

Zooey stopped straining against her constraints and laid her head back against the lumpy pillow. It was becoming clear she wasn't going to get any answers until she provided some for them. She held back her tears and swallowed the lump in her throat. With a pitiful attempt, she rubbed each cheek on her shoulder to dry them.

"I had just gotten off work—H&M—and I was walking to the train." Her voice shook, but she pressed on for the sake of figuring things out. "It had to be about 10:30 at night. I'd had a rough day and was feeling a little stressed, so I decided at the last minute to take a lap around the Common first to clear my head.

"Talk of the cure and safer streets had been going around. I thought I would be okay." Her vision blurred as tears collected in her eyes again. She could see her words played out like a movie in her head as she spoke. "I was attacked by the gazebo, bit on the shoulder. I didn't see it coming, and I couldn't get away..." she swallowed and her breath hitched in her chest. "And then everything went black. That's all I can remember."

The doctor didn't write any of this down. He simply stared into Zooey's dull-gray eyes as if she were the only other person on the planet at that moment, his head continually nodding like a bobble.

"And do you remember what the date was when this happened?"

Zooey's eyes shifted from his to the nurse's and back. Her stomach tightened. "Umm..." she sniffed to stay in control of herself. "May twenty-first," she finally said. "Why? How long did it take for you to find me? My roommate must have called when I didn't come home. Was it last night? Two nights ago?"

The doctor wiped his face with the palm of his hand, brushing back his short hair, and then leaned back in the chair. "It's July seventeenth," he said painfully. "You've been gone for almost two months."

She felt like she'd been punched in the gut. Zooey tried to take in a breath, but it was nearly impossible. Her chest heaved violently as she wheezed. The machine next to her bed beeped wildly and the nurse leaned over to turn it off.

"How can I lose two months of my life and not remember anything?"

The doctor continued to explain the situation. "Even though the cure is out there, we have not been able to capture and treat every single zombie in the United States yet. This is an ongoing problem because as we cure a handful, another handful is created by the ones still out there, as in your case."

Tears flooded Zooey's eyes and cascaded down her pale cheeks. The salt stung at her wounds, but she couldn't stop. She was one of them—a monster, a living nightmare, a cannibal!

"Does that mean I-I-I killed…people?" she sobbed, wanting desperately to cover her face with her hands as she struggled against the handcuffs again.

They dug into her flesh, tearing away at her already tender skin. She flung her head to the side in an attempt to hide her scrunched-up face.

"Now, now, we can't be sure what happened," Doctor Fullerton said in a soothing voice as he stroked her hair. "All we know is that you are human again and your life can be restored to what it once was with a little help. Would you like that?"

The sweet, placid tone of his voice seeped in through Zooey's ears and calmed her firing nerves. Her chest slowly stopped racking as she looked up into his kind eyes. She sniffed back her tears and used her shoulders to wipe her cheeks again. As she brushed the right one, a sharp pain made her wince.

"What do I do now?" she asked, meek and defeated.

Doctor Fullerton sighed through his slim nose. "For starters, you'll have to stay here for a total of three weeks, assuming nothing else comes up medically. We did have to stitch you up a bit due to some substantial lacerations on your face and shoulder. Luckily, none of it required any surgery or skin grafting."

Zooey nodded delicately. All she wanted in that moment was a mirror. The pain in her face doubled as she wondered how closely she resembled Frankenstein's monster. She didn't notice the nurse, who moved like a ghost to stand next to her, an empty syringe in his hand.

The doctor continued to outline her stay as her thoughts drifted in and out. "You will have one more day in this room to sleep off the sedative. You have already been out for two days so one more should suffice. After that, you'll be moved into the Adult

Undead Ward. There you will attend group counseling and one-on-one sessions with me daily to make sure we are preparing you for the outside world again. How does that sound?"

Zooey sat in silence as she took it all in. Her head felt heavy, like a bowling ball on a stick. "And once I'm released? What happens then?" she managed to slur.

The doctor smiled with a row of straight white teeth beaming out to her. She flinched at the sight of them.

"Great question! Well, you will continue to see me every two weeks for your treatment and a thirty minute therapy session to make sure you're acclimating okay. Those only last for the first year and then you can go to one of the many walk-in clinics that are being trained on how to administer the treatment on-site."

Her eyes drifted over to the male nurse who now hovered in the corner behind the doctor. She looked to her left where he had been standing a moment ago in disbelief. She slowly moved her head to stare at him again. He folded his arms and tightened the muscles in his face. A chill ran down her spine and she shivered.

She let her eyes wander the room to avoid the nurse's gaze. There were three white padded walls and one glass one. Outside the room, she saw someone in a blue jumpsuit sitting in a rolling chair identical to the doctor's and another younger man in a blue jumpsuit with orange hair standing next to him. There was something familiar about those two, but she couldn't put her finger on it.

"Does that sound good to you, Miss Beckett?"

She turned her gaze to the doctor again. He looked into her eyes deeply, as if in desperate anticipation of her agreement. His eyes briefly shifted to the nurse in the corner, whose jaw clenched in the heavy silence.

"Sure," she said. "Sound good."

"Excellent," he breathed out with a smile. "Then all that's left is the interview." He pulled a small notebook out from his pocket, along with a ballpoint pen. "What is your full name?"

Her eyes closed in a slow blink, almost too heavy to open again. Whatever the nurse had given her was strong. "Zooey Marie Beckett."

"And when is your birthdate?"

"December 1, 1990."

The doctor nodded his head as his pen scribbled away. "So that makes you twenty-six now," he said more to himself. "And what is your occupation? Retail, or did you hold other jobs aside from H&M?"

Zooey blinked slowly several more times. Her head was foggy as it adjusted from being dead to alive again, fighting through the sedative.

"I was supposed to start Grad School for psychology at Harvard, but the school closed after the outbreak. I was only working at H&M as a part-time job to make rent, well until the landlord disappeared. Then, I was working for food mostly."

She could hear herself rambling, but her lips wouldn't stop moving.

"Ah, Harvard!" the doctor bellowed as he uncrossed his legs to switch them. "You plan to finish your degree then?"

She readjusted herself to sit up as much as she could without disturbing the handcuffs. "I'm not sure. I'm not sure about anything really." Her gaze glazed over as the weight of her new life crashed down on her.

Doctor Fullerton waved the question away with his pen. "Don't worry about. That's what the counseling sessions are for. Now, are you originally from Boston?"

"No. My family lives in…Walker's Landing… Washington." Her words stumbled over one another as her lips started to tingle.

There was no hint of recognition on the doctor's face. She wasn't surprised. Her hometown wasn't close to any major cities. If he wasn't big into fishing as a profession, it was unlikely he would have ever heard of the place.

"And tell me about your family."

"Why?" she forced out harshly. "I haven't lived with them in eight years. I barely speak to them."

"Okay, tell me about who you do live with then," the doctor said without missing a beat.

Zooey's eyes finally closed for good as she thought about her roommate. A warmth spread through her chest as she pictured Elizabeth standing at the kitchen counter sipping from one of her oversized coffee mugs, tapping her foot. She was always tapping her foot.

"Her name is Elizabeth Wentworth. She graduated from Harvard with me and was supposed to begin Law School before all this." Her voice was slow, calculated, and distant.

"Quite an ambitious pair you two make."

Zooey smiled, feeling a sharp pinch in her right cheek. Instinct made her hand shoot up to touch it in comfort, yanking the handcuffs against the railing again. The nurse in the corner unfolded his arms and took a step forward, but Doctor Fullerton held a hand up.

"Can you loosen these?" Zooey asked. "Or take one off so I can scratch my nose if I want to?" One of her droopy eyes cracked open.

The doctor's gaze softened on her. "I wish I could, but we have to keep them on for a full seventy-two hours. It's hospital policy."

Zooey let out a frustrated huff and let her eyes close again.

"Do you mind me asking why you don't speak to your family anymore?"

Her dark brows pulled together as her forehead wrinkled. "I still talk to them, just not much," she corrected him. "My parents are stuck in a loveless marriage and they feel they have to make life miserable for everyone around them. My younger brother is a drug addict, in and out of rehab."

The doctor didn't say anything. He wrote on his small pad of paper furiously with his own forehead wrinkled in concentration.

"I think I've got just about all I need," he said with a smile, and he stood up. "You rest as best you can and tomorrow morning we will have you moved to a more permanent room."

He laid a hand gently on her upper arm. Her first instinct was to shrink away. She didn't know this man at all apart from his name and profession. But the longer his touch lingered, the more she relaxed into it. It'd been almost two months since she had any living human contact. Though her brain couldn't remember this, her body seemed to. She took a deep breath and let it out slowly through her nostrils, relaxing her muscles and mind as she gave into the heavy sedative.

"Can I call Elizabeth and tell her I'm all right?" she forced out before unconsciousness took hold of her.

At this, the doctor removed his hand and placed it in the pocket of his jeans. "I'm afraid you're not allowed to make any phone calls yet. We are still preparing you for rehabilitation, and we have to prepare your roommate as well."

Her lids wrenched open and she stared into his baby blue eyes, hoping she could telepathically wear him down into breaking the rules just this once. It didn't work. He simply stared back sympathetically, his eyes turned upward like a damaged puppy dog.

"It'll get better, Miss Beckett. Just give it time," he said as he turned for the door. "Everything will be back to normal before you know it."

That was the first lie Doctor Fullerton told Zooey Beckett.

Chapter Three

Zooey shambled through the Boston Common, one foot dragging behind the other. She gave a drawn-out groan. There was no one else with her. The twinkling of stars and the big, crescent moon guided her through the trees.

Desire burned in her till she felt physical pain throughout her body. She needed brains badly. Her high had worn off from the last time she ate and all she was left with was a hollowness inside. There had to be someone, anyone, walking around on this warm summer night to eat.

As if in answer to her prayers, a young man in tight shorts and a tank-top jogged around the corner. The white wires to his earbuds bounced against his chest as he breathed steadily.

Zooey watched from behind a tree. He was headed her way. All she would have to do is wait for the right moment and throw herself onto him. With every stride he came closer to the horrific, bloody death awaiting him.

She gnawed at her bottom lip in anticipation. His yummy, gooey, dripping brain was all she could think about. She had to have them.

Just as the jogger rounded the turn in the pathway, Zooey lunged from the shadows to tackle him to the ground. Before he could let out his first cry, she sunk her teeth into his arm. It wasn't that she wanted to eat his flesh. That would only temporarily satisfy her craving. Biting him debilitated him, distracted him, while she worked at splitting open his hard head to suck out the juicy morsels inside.

Blood rushed over her tongue as she tore through his muscles. The man let out a shriek that seemed to split the night in two. She pulled herself on top of him, pinning him as he fought back with his good arm. Each blow to her head felt like he was hitting her with a foam swimming noodle. It did nothing to deter her, and certainly didn't make her give up. Nothing would. She had to have those brains.

Sinking her teeth into his tender neck, she ripped out his Adam's apple. Arterial blood sprayed upward like a fountain as the man relaxed onto the pavement with his eyes wide open. He didn't struggle against her anymore.

Zooey's face was drenched and warm. She licked her lips clean and her eyes rolled back into her head. She was thankful there were no other zombies nearby. Sharing the brains she worked so hard to get would have been a bummer.

She held the man's face in both her hands, lifting his head up from the sidewalk. His mouth was open, his handsome, young face forever petrified with a look of horror. He looked about the same age as Zooey. She wondered if he was a Harvard student like her, killing time until school reopened its doors so he could get on with his life.

With force, she threw his head down. A loud crack echoed off the trees. She did this over and over again until the back of his head was nothing more than a bloody mess of broken skull and leaking fluids. She dug her fingers into the cracks and ripped apart to reveal the treasure inside—his brain.

She scooped out the large pink muscle delicately. It was heavier than most of the brains she ate. Inside she smiled, though the muscles in her face wouldn't mimic the feeling. She turned the brain over in her hands, looking at it from all angles. It was a mighty fine brain, indeed.

With the ravenous force of a starved jackal, she shoved it into her mouth and tore off a large chunk. Blood and fluid slathered down her chin as she chewed. Warmth spread through her throat, and then her stomach. Her own brain lit up as if someone had turned on a lightswitch inside her head. Memories of going out with Elizabeth and Oliver played before her eyes like a movie, bringing back all the wonderful feelings that went along with them. Her body didn't feel like deadweight being dragged around anymore. Instead, it felt light as a feather, as if she would float away in the next breeze.

She swallowed the bits in her mouth and then dove forward for another bite.

Zooey shot upward, but was pulled back by the handcuffs still locked around her wrists. The lights had been turned on, glaring down at her like an extraterrestrial beam. She squinted her eyes until they were able to adjust.

"Time to get up," a gruff woman's voice called as she yanked the covers back.

Zooey's legs shrank under her for warmth. She was drenched in sweat and shivering.

The large woman, on her last leg of middle-age, went through the robotic routine of shutting off all the machines without glancing in Zooey's direction.

Finally, able to open her eyes, she saw the nurse bend down to unlock her cuffs. The sweet release felt like a hundred pounds lifted. Zooey sat upright and wrapped her arms around her waist, both for warmth and comfort. Her matted hair scratched sorely.

"Get up!" the woman barked.

Zooey noticed a hulking man in a security officer's uniform standing in the corner by the door. He was at least six-foot-five with rippling muscles that stretched the black fabric of his uniform to the breaking point. Not a single emotion could be recognized on his tanned face. But it was the squatty nurse that made Zooey flinch. She had the face of a bulldog and a bite that was worse.

"Do you want to be moved to your own room or not, girl?"

"My name's Zooey," she said under her breath.

She swung her legs over the edge of the bed slowly and let her bare feet touch the cold floor. The urge to pull back was almost more than she could bear. Now that her hands were free, all she wanted to do was curl up into a ball and sleep for a week.

A brisk shove on her back forced her to stand.

"On your feet, Undead."

"Undead?" Zooey wondered aloud as she moved forward.

The nurse handed her a ratty blue robe and then strode out the door. Officer Ferrigno held his hand out, signaling her to follow. She put the robe on and wrapped it tightly around her thin frame.

"After you," he said politely.

All she could do was let them herd her from one room to another like a little lost sheep.

As she walked down the deserted hallway, watching the oversized hips of Nurse Crabapple swing back and forth grotesquely, she thought about the nightmare she'd had.

She ate some poor guy's brains. First she killed him, ripped his throat out with her teeth like a maniac, and then proceeded to bash his head in and eat his brains. The psychologist in her tried to rationalize it away as a dream, but she wasn't entirely convinced.

The long, empty corridor seemed to extend forever. Each time they went through a set of doors, they continued down another hallway to another set with no end in sight.

She glanced through a window into one of the many rooms lining the walls. Her pace slowed as she tried to get a good look at who was inside. Then, she stopped. A lonely man sat in a wheelchair by the window overlooking the rooftop. He had no hair on half his head and a big scar with stitches and staples running down the other side, weaving through his sparse brown strands. His face had been pieced back together and resembled a Halloween mask. She wasn't sure if he could see her through the puffiness of his eyes, though he turned to face her listlessly and then back to the window.

A lump moved up through Zooey's throat. She hadn't seen herself in a mirror yet and was unable to get a good look at her reflection in any of the windows. If she looked anything like the man in the wheelchair, then they must have pumped some good drugs into her. On a whole, she didn't feel that bad. Her breathing quickened anyhow.

"Let's go, Miss," the officer said as he approached her and invaded her personal space.

She moved to catch up to the rotund nurse still leading the way. Her right ankle was starting to sting with every step she took. It had been wrapped tightly in a bloody bandage. She cringed at the thought of what was hidden under the dressing. It couldn't be anything good. To avoid thinking about it, she let her mind wander, hoping it would take her to a happier place, but her thoughts turned back to her slurping the gooey brains of the guy she killed.

"In here," the nurse barked as she opened a door that looked like all the rest. The plaque next to it read 'decontamination room'. "Let's clean you up before we toss you in with the rest."

Zooey's eyes darted from the nurse to the door. There was a churning in her stomach, a deep instinct that told her not to go in there. But the nurse narrowed her eyes and grit her teeth the longer Zooey stood. Finally, the woman gave her a swift shove on the shoulder, pushing her inside.

"Get in that tub."

The room was completely empty aside from a large metal tub that looked like it had been a pig trough in its former life. Zooey pulled her robe tighter around her waist.

"Strip down and get in!" the nurse yelled in a voice fitting of a large man.

It made Zooey jump, goosebumps running down her arms. She slowly undid the tie of the robe and slid it from her shoulders.

"I won't bite," the nurse said as she gathered several towels and laid them down on the wet floor.

She cackled like a witch stoking the fire beneath her cauldron.

Zooey's eyes widened. This woman was insane. She took pleasure in pushing around former zombies like they weren't human beings anymore. Zooey wondered if that was how the rest of the world would view her, as some rotting sack of meat that used to be dead.

She pulled down her thin hospital pants and slipped her top off over her head. As the scratchy material grazed her right shoulder, she felt a pinch and then a pull. She looked down at herself to inspect the damage.

The nurse huffed as she plopped down onto a wooden chair next to the tub. The legs groaned under her weight. "I don't have all day to wait for you to admire yourself. Let's go!"

On the tips of her toes, Zooey walked over slowly. She lowered herself into the basin, her eyes turned up as she tried to cover as much of her naked body as she could with her hands. As soon as her bare skin touched the cold, stainless steel, the urge to pee struck her.

"I have to use the bathroom," she said meekly, avoiding eye contact.

"Go in the tub."

The nurse dunked a sponge into a small pale at her feet and squeezed the excess water out. She slapped it onto Zooey's back as if she were scrubbing the grime from a toilet.

"Jesus! That's freezing!"

"Lotta Undead to clean. We don't always have time to draw a warm bath and light candles for you all."

Zooey wrinkled her nose, but in the end she had no choice. Warm liquid rushed out from between her legs and pooled around her bottom as she sat with her knees pulled into her chest. Her urine was black. Zooey tried not to look. She closed her eyes and let the nurse scrub away her sins.

"Disgusting…filthy…undead…" the nurse grumbled, avoiding the stitches just barely.

There was nothing Zooey could do but accept that she had to receive a sponge-bath from Nurse

Trunchbull while sitting in her own waste, shivering, sweating, and starving. Her head fell to rest on her shoulder. The texture of her skin was rough and uneven. Slowly, she looked down and then screamed out, causing the nurse to jump back and fall out of her chair.

The tender part where her neck met her shoulder was missing a large chunk. The skin was a sickly mixture of red, blue, purple, and yellow. It looked like the marks of a wild animal, but she knew it was human teeth that had sunk into her flesh and tore it away.

Suddenly, her stomach lurched upward. She tried to cover her mouth, but the bile rose too quickly and splayed out on the floor as the nurse righted herself to sit on the chair again.

"Vile creatures," the nurse said with her nose wrinkled.

Zooey could feel her cheeks burn with embarrassment as the stench of her vomit filled the room.

"Stand up," the nurse ordered after a minute.

Zooey did so without hesitation this time. The woman scrubbed off every last bit of blood, dirt, urine, and anything else that clung to her skin. She tossed the last of the freezing water over Zooey's head without warning.

Naked and shaking uncontrollably, Zooey hugged herself as towels were hurled at her. *I'm a Harvard graduate, Goddammit,* she thought as she dried herself off.

But the nurse didn't care if she was the Pope himself. All she saw when she looked at Zooey was an abomination. This wasn't something that had to be said. Every single time their eyes met, Zooey saw the hatred that lie not so far beneath the surface.

Chapter Four

Zooey finally made it to her room. When she got there, a young girl with long, curly, auburn hair was lying in bed, her back facing the door. The nurse flicked on the lightswitch, as she'd done to Zooey earlier that morning, and called out to the motionless body.

"Get up, lazy! Time for breakfast. Wash your face, wipe your ass, and let's go!"

The girl stirred, stretched her arms over her head, and finally turned to stare at the ceiling. Her face was pale, but the heavy splatter of freckles gave the illusion of warmth.

"Hi," she said in a voice thick with sleep.

Zooey let her lips pull up into a smile that refused to reach her eyes. She was still reeling over her morning sponge bath.

"Get in there," the nurse said, pointing to the bathroom. "Have a look at yourself, cry about it, and then go eat something."

Zooey's face pulled together in disdain. What was that woman doing working in the Undead Ward if she felt such blatant disgust for them all? Was there no standards to who they hired? She felt the sudden urge to tell her best friend, Elizabeth, all about the horrible woman. You could bet something would be done about the lack of compassion around there quick. Elizabeth had a voice that couldn't be ignored and a burning desire to help the less fortunate, which now included Zooey.

Though the urge to disobey was there, Zooey walked into the tiny bathroom and shut the door behind her. She had to see what the last two months had done to her—how it had changed her forever. She stood in front of the small rectangular mirror and flicked the lights on.

Her breath caught in her chest as a solid mass sank into the pit of her stomach. Her long, brown hair was matted into clumps. She pulled it back behind her shoulders to get a better look at her scarred face. Deep scratches ran along both sides of her head, creeping down into her cheeks and jawline. Most seemed superficial, but one was so deep it had to be sewn shut. The contrast of the black thread against her sickly pale skin made the hair on the back of her neck stand on end. Her flesh was red and swollen around each entry point.

She leaned in closer and noticed her eyes had even changed color. Once a brilliant shade of sapphire, they now were the same dull gray as spoiled meat. The purple bags underneath and her protruding cheek bones made the look sunken. Her lip quivered. She barely recognized herself. Before tears could form, she shut the light off and went back into her sleeping quarters.

Her roommate was now sitting up on the bed, her bare toes wiggling back to life.

"I still wake up pretty stiff in the mornings," the girl said casually.

Zooey didn't realize she was staring from the bathroom doorway.

The girl looked up with a sad smile. A scar ran up from the left side of her mouth to the corner of her eye. It was deep and purple, stapled together sloppily. White bandages wrapped around her neck, red seeping through on all sides. Her exposed arms were ravaged with various degrees of cuts and bites.

Zooey opened her mouth to say something in return, but was at a loss for words. She was grateful she walked away with the minimal damage she had.

As if reading her mind, the girl stood up and said, "You must not have been out there long. You don't look too beat up." When Zooey still didn't say anything, the girl continued. "My name's Chastity. Chastity Grace." She gave an embarrassed, breathy laugh as she took a step forward. She was twenty-four-years-old, but only looked to be about seventeen. "My parents are super religious. Do you want to sit with me at breakfast?"

Still unable to utter a single word, Zooey nodded her head and followed the red-haired girl out into the common area where a long table with a dozen metal chairs sat around it. Several of the other in-house patients had already been served their morning meal—dry toast, watered-down scrambled eggs, and burnt sausage links. Most stared past their food, pushing it around with a plastic spork.

Zooey sat down carefully and folded her hands in her lap. She felt awkward and out of place. The other patients looked ten times worse off than she did. It made her feel grateful and ashamed at the same time, like her mere presence was saying to the others "I'm sure glad I don't look as bad as you!"

A tray was set in front of her by a young male nurse in green scrubs. Her stomach growled, but she had no desire to eat the food. Images of her chin slathered in fresh blood still lingered in her mind. The scrambled eggs too closely resembled the brain matter that spilled out on the dark pavement.

"We got another live one!" she heard a booming voice call out from across the table.

The man laughed, his red, round face wrinkled with angry scarring. He was in his early forties with short black hair and thin blue-ish gray eyes. His large stomach pressed up against the edge of the table, partially resting on top for support.

"Name's David Stern," he said, shoveling sausage into his mouth. "If you don't think you'll eat your breakfast, I'd be happy to take it off your hands."

Zooey eyed him and then shoved the tray across the table. Without hesitation, he scooped the food onto his own tray and shoved it back to her.

"We're not supposed to share, but I think it's a waste not to. They just throw it away if we don't eat it."

She wasn't looking for an explanation. Under normal circumstances, she would have agreed, but today was anything but normal. Her mind was still stuck on the images of her eating the jogger, wondering if it was just a dream or a forgotten memory from her lost two months.

Next to David Stern was a young man, freshly twenty, with a brown afro and a freckled nose, or what was left of it. The entire right side of his face looked as if it had been pieced back together quickly, covered with skin from other parts of his body. Looking at it made Zooey's stomach queasy. Her eyes turned away with guilt.

A few seats down, a girl in her mid-twenties with brown skin and grown out pastel silver extensions stabbed at her food. Between jabs she eyed David Stern as if she wished the eggs were his face.

Another body plopped down in the seat next to Zooey, yanking her out of her self-pitying daydreams. She looked over from the corner of her eye. There was something familiar about him.

"You look like shit," he said.

Her eyes narrowed as she looked around to see if he was talking to someone else.

He turned to face her. His clean-shaven face revealed superficial scratches along his jawline. The side of his head was shaved where they had to staple together torn skin. Clearly, someone had tried to get at his brains.

"Don't tell me you've forgotten all those beautiful memories we shared together," he whispered, leaning in close.

The scarring around his full lips did nothing to dampen the charm of his smile.

Zooey stared, lost.

"For the best," he said, turning back to the plate in front of him and taking a bite. "Don't want to let them know you remember anything from before."

He shoveled in his eggs, not stopping to chew before he swallowed. His thin fingers grasped the spork desperately, shaking with each raise to his mouth.

"I think…" she began, and then lowered her voice. "I think I do remember you," she whispered. "From the Common. We were brought in together, right?"

His hand lowered to the tray, hovering an inch over it. "That's right. Have you been having dreams too?"

Zooey's eyes widened. Finally, some answers!

"Yes!" she said a little too loudly.

One of the nurses supervising the meal craned his neck to get a look at her. She lowered her face to stare into her plate, her long ratty hair hiding her briefly.

"These dreams…did they really happen? Did I really do those things?" She tried to hide the panic in her voice, but it crept in through high notes.

"If I said yes, would you be able to handle it?"

Her mouth fell open as she stared at the man. Whatever he'd done as a zombie, it didn't seem to eat away at him like it did her. She wondered how anyone could live with themselves after what they'd done. How was she going to?

Horror-stricken remorse must have shown on her face, because the man quickly turned his whole body to her and took her hands in his.

"No, no, don't worry. Please. I didn't mean to upset you. I just thought since we have a history, maybe it'd be nice to get to know each other, talk about what happened, help each other get through this alive."

A tear slid down her broken cheek. The man reached up gently and wiped it away. He lowered his face to gaze into her wet eyes, waiting for her to speak.

She looked at him, really looked at him, and felt a connection. There was a familiarity about him that only came from knowing one another deeply. Sharing brains had to be a deeply intimate act for zombies. Her cheeks blushed and she turned away.

"I was hoping it was all a dream, that I—"

"Wandered the Common alone, not harming a single person?" He gave a breathy, sad-soaked laugh. "We all wish for that. But we have to face the truth about what really happened, or we'll never be able to move on."

She nodded her head and looked down at his hands around hers.

"I'm Ren," he says. "Last name unknown. Everything is still a bit foggy up here." He pointed to his head partially covered in chestnut hair. "Weird how some things come back to us and some don't."

Zooey slowly moved her hands out from under his and took hold of her spork, forgetting that David Stern had eaten all her food already. The overweight man was yacking to the kid next to him about his days on the railway and how much money he used to make as a conductor.

"Which doctor did you get?" Ren asked, turning in his chair again to face forward.

"Dr. Fullerton."

"Ah," he said with a smile. "You've got yourself a good one—unprejudiced, nice bedside manner, not against handing out the prescriptions. They say he sympathizes with us because his wife Turned. He thinks she's still out there and one day they'll haul her in to be cured."

"How do you know so much about this place?" Zooey looked at him with a hunger in her eyes.

"I'm resourceful," he said with a coy smile.

Chapter Five

After breakfast, the group of ten was herded into the common room's sitting area, which consisted of hand-me-down sofas and armchairs. A flatscreen television hung on the green wall above one of the long bookshelves riddled with old TV guides and romance novels.

"Since we have newcomers, let's start off by going around the room and telling everyone your name, how long you've been here, and how long you were out there. I'll start. My name's Shawn. I came to work in the Undead Ward when it opened earlier this year," the muscular nurse with a clipboard said robotically.

"I'm Devin and I started here last month," the tall, thin one next to Shawn said. His eyes moved ceaselessly as he scanned the Undead sitting, staring at him.

Nurse Shawn looked to the next person to continue the meet-and-greet.

David Stern had a large armchair all to himself, mostly out of necessity. He talked loudly to anyone who would listen, which for the most part was no one. His face wasn't too badly wounded, only red superficial scratches on the surface, but both his arms were covered in white bandages.

"My name is David. I've been here for three days, and I was out there for a month."

Next to him on a tattered yellow loveseat was a slightly overweight woman with straw-colored hair resting on her shoulders. Zooey could see the ends of a long, ragged scar poking out of the collar of her shirt, almost in the same place Zooey's was. The woman kept looking at the desk where a phone sat in plain view. Her hands wrung together continuously.

"My name's Shelly Johnson. I got here two days ago and they still haven't let me call my family to make sure my kids are okay!" she said with a rising voice.

Shawn gave her a stern look with his angular jaw clenched that told her she had better move on.

"I was out there for ten weeks," she said with her eyes turned down.

On the other side of the loveseat was the young boy with the large, curly hair and mangled face she'd seen talking to David at breakfast. He stretched his long, thin legs out to the middle of the floor and leaned back as far as he could into the cushions. His hands were folded over his stomach, his chest breathing in and out slowly. Zooey wasn't sure if he was relaxing, or if he was in some deep state of meditation in a feeble attempt to maintain his sanity.

Without opening his eyes he said, "I'm Derek Lawson. I've been here a week already thanks to all the surgery. I was out there for four months."

Zooey had to work hard to keep her eyes from bulging, but it was all in vain as her lips parted and her mouth hung open. No wonder the poor kid needed so much work done. He'd been bit, clawed, and torn apart for twice as long as she had. The things he must have seen, must have done. If she were him, she wouldn't be able to open her eyes to look at anyone else either.

To her left sat Ren—cool, calm, and collected. He looked as if he didn't have a care in the world, though he'd so recently murdered and consumed people. The very thought made Zooey want to rip her own hair out and eat it.

"My name is Ren. I can't remember my last name at the moment so you can just use Undead for now. I was brought here three days ago and I was out there for, gosh, six months I think?"

He looked to Zooey, as if for confirmation. She simply stared back at him in unabashed shock.

"It's your turn, Zooey," he said, pulling her out of her mind.

She blinked and looked out to the others. "Right. I'm Zooey Beckett. I've been here three days as well and I was out there for almost two months." She spoke quickly and then looked to Chastity, who sat with her hands in her lap and her head down, unable to meet the gaze of anyone else in the room.

Her fingers reached up to her neck, as if to twirl the ghost of a necklace she'd long since lost. Her green eyes seemed to grow darker as she realized nothing was there.

"Hello. My name's Chastity Grace. I've been here five days, and I was out there for three-and-a-half months."

By now, everyone was getting bored. The heap of an old man in the armchair next to Chasity snorted, hunched over and sour-faced. Deep scars mixed with the lines of his wrinkles. His thin, dull eyes judged each and every Undead as if he hadn't devoured a single rain while in his zombie state.

"Name's Benjamin Tat and no you may not call me Ben, Benji, or Benny. Just Benjamin, Mr. Tat, or Sir." He turned his stern gaze to the two nurses standing. "The same goes for you, too! I was hauled in here four days ago, and from what I can gather I was out there for six weeks or so." He threw his hands up in the air. "I don't know, so they tell me."

Ren nudged Zooey in the ribs and nodded knowingly to Benjamin, though she couldn't figure out why. He was just like any other cranky old man, aside from the whole former zombie thing.

The next to go was a young guy with sunken eyes, dirty-blonde, curly hair, and a tall, thin frame. He sat with a defiant smirk that said about as loud as it could that he didn't want to be there. A long, red scar ran from his forehead, over his missing eye, and down his sharp jawline. Acne still riddled his uneven skin, though it seemed to have bigger problems now. The stitches stuck out sorely. If they hadn't been in place, Zooey was sure she could easily part his pale skin to get a peek at what was underneath, a thought that sent her stomach lurching.

"I'm Sam Kyle and this whole group therapy thing you got going on here is bullshit." His one hazel eye glared straight at the nurses.

Shawn made a move toward Sam, but the cocky kid held his hands up in mock surrender.

"Okay, okay, I'll play nice. I was brought here against my will four days ago. I was out there for five short months."

"I warned you about saying stuff like that," Nurse Shawn said with authority. He wrote something down on his chart, something he didn't do after anyone else spoke.

Devin stood in the background, watching intently in case he ever had to assume the role of nurse-in-charge. Zooey could tell by the tension in his hunched shoulders that he hoped that day would never come. His soft eyes met hers and he quickly looked away.

"Anymore comments like that from you and you're out," the nurse warned with a point of his pen.

Sam waved his hands through the air. "Ooo," he laughed before placing them behind his head to lean back.

Next to him on the loveseat was the young black woman with silver hair. Her arms folded over her large chest to hide the hideous scar running down between her breasts. Long, white marks plagued the creamy, dark skin along her arms, shoulders, neck, and face. Stitches seemed to be the only thing holding her together at the moment.

"I'm Tamara Knox. I came here five days ago, I was only out there for four, and I don't understand why I gotta stay here longer than I was zombified out there. It makes no goddamn sense. But that's my reality now, so nice to meet y'all."

"Warning, Tamara," Shawn hissed, though there was no final count as there had been for Sam.

And finally, in an armchair all to herself was a small woman with choppy brown hair cut just above her shoulders. Flecks of green clung for life in her protruding eyes that darted from one Undead to the next.

"I'm Alissa," she said nervously. She raised her thumb to her mouth and bit on the nail. "I've been here almost a week and I was out there for eight months."

Zooey stared, looking the woman over for trauma. Surely there had to be something after being out there for so long, but all she saw were partially healed scratches and a nervous glint in her eye.

"We're going to watch a brief video and then we can start the group session," Shawn said as he grabbed the remote from the shelf under the television.

There was an audible groan from several of the seats.

"I know some of you have seen this already, but bear with me. We have quite a few new faces today."

He held up the remote and pressed play. Bouncy, outdated music blared as a cartoon doctor strolled jauntily onto the screen. He stopped, pretending to only notice in passing the audience sitting in front of him. With a quick swipe down his white labcoat, he smiled and started his spiel.

Nurse Shawn settled into a folding chair at the back of the group and pulled out his phone covertly to check his text messages.

"Hello, there!" the doctor's voice was as upbeat as the xylophone that played in the background. "And welcome back. Some of you have been gone for quite a while, haven't you? Why don't we catch you up on all that's happened?"

Zooey looked from Ren to Chastity, her forehead wrinkled.

"Back in the summer of 2012 a new plague ravished the world. For lack of a better term, it was deemed the 'zombie plague', and rightfully so, I should say! Walking, chomping, rotting corpses everywhere, more and more created with every infectious bite."

The Undead new to the Ward looked to each other in shock. Zooey couldn't believe the hospital would ever show something like this. It was insulting and degrading to everyone in the room, living or recently deceased.

"But what is the zombie plague? To put it simply, it is an infection in the blood, spread through fluids from zombie to living person. Yup, that's right!" the doctor said enthusiastically as he wiped his stethoscope on the bottom of his jacket. "That means it is not only spread through bites and possibly scratches, but also through intercourse, so think twice before you jump into bed with a normal human being. They could wake up…a zombie!" He raised his hands and groaned mockingly.

"*Normal* human beings?" Zooey barked aloud.

Everyone froze in their seats. Ren nudged her in the side and glared with wide eyes. The two nurses barely glanced from the screen, but she saw the muscles in Shawn's jaw tighten. Devin pretended he hadn't heard, but his eyes shifted between her and the other nurse as if he were waiting for his co-worker to lunge at the outspoken woman. He gave her a quick smile and then turned his head back to watch the screen. Zooey's jaw clamped shut.

"The plague spread quickly, but the police and military were on top of it. Cities carried on and people were protected. Slowly, the number of zombies diminished as zombie eradication teams were dispatched, but it was impossible to clear them from the population entirely…that is, until the creation of Zombutexachlorepinol!"

The long, complicated name flashed like a neon sign above the cartoon doctor's head. Then, a bright green, groaning, moaning, stereotypical zombie, sloppily drawn and stupid-looking, shuffled into view. The doctor whipped out a giant syringe from behind his back and stuck it in the zombie's arm. Instantly, the monster changed back into a functional human being with wavy blonde hair and dimples. There wasn't a scratch on him.

Zooey huffed between her lips and then quickly straightened herself up in her seat. Her eyes shifted nervously around the room. No one seemed to notice.

"Welcome back, Stan!" the doctor said, clapping the man on the back.

"Good to be back, doc!" Stan's teeth shone with a bright twinkle when he smiled.

Zooey had been too preoccupied with the scars on her face to look, but from the gritty feeling when she rolled her tongue over her own teeth she was sure they were anything but sparkling. At least they were all still there, unlike David Stern, Derek Lawson, and Sam Kyle. Each had their own unique jack-o-lantern smile.

"Z-shots are administered bi-weekly, on the dot, no exceptions. So, no skipping out to go on a hot date with your new Undead girlfriend," the doctor winked at Stan, who miraculously now had a busty blonde holding onto his arm. "Wherever you were administered your first shot is where you will continue to have your bi-weekly shots indefinitely. Not from there, you say? That's okay! Get a job, buy a house, and ship the little missus and the kids out to be with you. Your health is our number one concern."

Chastity, Sam, and Alissa were the only ones who sat upright at this, their eyes ready to pop out of their skulls. Zooey wasn't from Boston, but she'd called it home for almost a decade now. She had no problem coming to the hospital every two weeks if it would keep her from turning into a brain-craving cannibal again. But those three obviously had somewhere else they'd rather be with families they wanted to get home to.

There was a pang in her chest as she watched the three sink into their chair, eyes distant and wet.

"Say, Stan, what have you been up to all this time anyway?"

Stan scratched his head like a caveman as he looked up at the top of the screen. "Gee, I can't remember. Is that normal, doc?"

The doctor walked forward to speak to the audience. "It's completely normal for you not to remember anything from when you were a zombie. While the drug works to repair the body back to a living, functional state, it cannot bring back the memories of that time. Brain function is at its lowest during the zombie state. But if you feel you are seeing images from then, whether awake or in your sleep, please let your doctor know right away."

"So, they can put you to sleep like a stray dog," Ren whispered into Zooey's ear.

His hot breath warmed her neck. On instinct, she leaned away and cringed her shoulders. She didn't know why that was her reaction. It wouldn't have been before.

"Thanks to Zombutexachlorepinol, a zombie is cured every five minutes in the United States alone.

The projection for complete extinction of the walking dead is only months away."

"That's great to hear, doc," Stan chimed in. "But what now?"

"I'm glad you asked, kiddo!" the doctor smiled and raised his eyebrows knowingly. "You are currently in one of the many Undead facilities across the country. Upon admittance, you were administered your first shot of Zombutexachlorepinol, more commonly referred to as the Z-shot. Most likely, our doctors mixed this with a heavy sedative to avoid shocking the system while it recovered itself back to life."

"WOW!" Stan exclaimed as he jumped impossibly in the air. "That's amazing!"

"It sure is, Stan. It sure is." the doctor fluffed the Undead guy's hair like he was a child at a baseball game. "During your three week stay, you will join doctors, nurses, and your fellow Undead in group activities, as well as one-on-one counseling to make sure you're acclimating to human life again."

Alissa waved her hand to get the attention of the two nurses, and then pointed to her room, mouthing that she had to use the restroom. Shawn rolled his eyes and nodded his head for her to get on with it before turning his attention back to his phone. She sped across the room without making a sound, closing the door behind her.

The video continued on about group therapy, doctor-patient counseling, psych evaluations, fitness, diet, and other innate things that would soon fill their days. Before, three weeks would have flown by as Zooey studied for final exams, went out to lunch in between classes with Elizabeth, and spent her weekends watching Oliver sing at open mic night in a local bar. Now, it seemed like an eternity. The walls were closing in on her as she sat there watching the cartoon doctor leer at her like a nightmare come to life.

When the video was finally over, Shawn and Devin stood at the front of the group again.

"Today we're going to go over how to approach your previous workplace to get your old job back if you so choose to. According to new laws to protect the Undead they cannot refuse you employment based on your condition or absence. They can, however, refuse you for other reasons, so be prepared."

Devin leaned over to Shawn and whispered something in his ear. He then walked over to Alissa's room and rapped on the door. When she didn't answer he let himself in. Shawn tried to continue with the lesson, but was interrupted almost immediately.

"Connelly, get in here!" he shouted.

The broad nurse dropped his clipboard and sprinted across the floor and into the room. "Jesus, not again," Zooey heard him mumble.

Everyone shifted in their chairs, to try to catch a peek at what was going on.

"What is it?" Zooey asked Ren and Chastity as they craned their necks.

"My guess is another suicide," Ren said casually.

Zooey's mouth fell open. "What? She was just here a few minutes ago! How could—"

"It happens more often than you think," Chastity said meekly.

Her chin met her chest as she whispered silent prayers for Alissa's departed soul.

Nurse Shawn walked backwards out of the room with his arms hooked under Alissa's. Devin had her by the ankles, struggling along. Zooey got a quick look as they walked the poor woman's limp body down the hallway and through a pair of black double doors.

Her neck was already black and blue from the bedsheets she used to hang herself with.

Ren leaned into Zooey to speak softly into her hair. "You go through those doors, you never come out again."

Chapter Six

After group therapy the Undead either went to meet with their physical trainers to work on strengthening their motor skills, or to their doctors for counseling. Zooey shuffled down the hall, past the desk in the common area, and around the corner to a closed door that read

Dr. Evan Fullerton
On-site Physician to the Undead

That word was really starting to piss Zooey off. Why did everyone else get to be normal human beings and she had to live the rest of her life as an Undead? Before the plague, people were pronounced clinically dead and then came back to life all the time. No one ever called them anything other than lucky.

She knocked on the door and waited with her arms folded tightly across her chest, fingers clenched around the ends of her thin hospital robe.

Doctor Fullerton opened the door with a smile. "Come on in, Zooey." He stood aside and held his arm out to welcome her.

His office was tiny, only big enough for a compact wooden desk, a few filing cabinets crammed behind it, and one chair for his patient. Despite its size, he kept the place tidy, not a single book or piece of paper out of place. The walls were as white as the hallways, so much so that they almost hurt Zooey's eyes if she looked at them for too long. There wasn't a single picture hanging anywhere.

She sat down in the hard chair and waited for him to arrange himself behind the desk. He swiveled his back to her and dug through one of the filing cabinets until he produced a thin manila envelope with her name on it.

Before he could say anything, Zooey spoke up, leaning forward in her seat. "Look, Doctor Fullerton, I appreciate you taking the time to see me, I really do. I know how helpful therapy can be for people with PTSD can be. Sometimes it's the only thing that seems to help them, but I don't have it. I can't even remember anything that happened. As far as I know I blacked out on the way home from work and woke up here."

There was a twinkle in his eyes as he stared at her. He bit down on the end of his pen and stared forward.

"All I really want is to call my family to tell them I'm okay and to make sure they're all okay and to see Elizabeth and Oliver."

The doctor sat up straight and wrote something down on the paper inside her file. "We have already contacted your family in Walker's Landing. They are all okay. None of them were infected, and they are glad to hear you have been cured. When you are home again they would like you to call them, but until then they feel it is best you focus on your recovery, and that includes one-on-one time with me."

He let this sink in with a moment of silence. Zooey stared at her hands as if she were being scolded by her dad. There was so much going on inside her head. She wished desperately that she could tell Doctor Fullerton all about it, but Ren was right. She should keep her memories of being a zombie to herself.

When she continued to sit quietly, the doctor continued. "As far as your roommate and friend, we have sent notice for them to visit you after your first week here is completed."

At that, Zooey's head rose and her eyes lit up. "Really?"

"Really," he said with a soft smile. "So, how about we utilize this hour to get to know each other a little better, figure out if there's anything beneficial you can get out of the time we have to spend together, hm?"

Zooey nodded her head as she allowed a grin to creep across her battered face.

"Good, now why don't we start with how you're feeling."

She shrugged her shoulders as she leaned back in the hard chair. "I feel fine."

Doctor Fullerton gave a quick snort and leaned across the desk. "Come on now. You're a psych student. You can do better than that, can't you?"

Zooey wanted to hate the Undead Ward and everyone in it. She thought the video they showed was wildly inappropriate and insensitive, the food was disgusting, the restrictions were equivalent to prison, and it seemed like everyone they hired was prescreened to make sure they had a healthy hatred for their patients—everyone except Doctor Fullerton, that is. He was the only one who genuinely seemed to want to help reintegrate the Undead back into society, and not just because the government said he had to. Zooey felt a deeply rooted respect for him, but that didn't make it any easier for her to open up to him.

"I still feel like myself. I don't really think anything has changed, except for the scarring on my face and body."

"Are you sure?"

She shrugged her shoulders again.

"I know you say you don't remember being a zombie, but I know you are well aware of what zombies are capable of, what they're known for doing to people."

She didn't nod her head this time, or move a single muscle. All she could do was stare down at her clasped hands. Her head screamed for him to change the subject, but her lips refused to move.

"You killed people, Zooey. How does that make you feel?"

A tear slid down her cheek as she let out a sharp huff from between her split lip. "How does it make me feel? How do you think it makes me feel?!" Her voice grew louder.

She didn't mean to yell at the doctor. He was only doing his job in asking her this. But the same images of her devouring the innocent jogger played in her mind like a bad horror movie, and the worst part was she couldn't tell anyone. How was she supposed to move on from the things she'd done if she couldn't talk about it?

She took a deep breath in, held it, and let it out slowly. "I feel sick to my stomach just thinking about it."

"Do you feel like you should be punished for your actions?"

He was poking around to see if she was going to kill herself like Alissa had done moments ago. She wanted to tell him he needn't worry. That she may feel disgusted by the things she did as a zombie, she may hate herself forever for it, but she planned on sticking around for a long time, if only to prove that the Undead were just as worthy of life as any other human being.

"I was sick. I didn't know what I was doing."

"When the mentally ill commit murder, they still have to go through trial, sometimes serve time, most likely in an institution of some sort to protect society from them harming anyone else."

A spark ignited in Zooey. It'd been so long since someone drudged up a healthy debate about anything that interested her. When Harvard closed its doors two years ago she felt like her intellect was being wasted on things like toilet paper rations and how to organize the pantry to hold to most amount of food. Survival was all she'd thought about for so long. She realized Doctor Fullerton wasn't asking these questions to be insensitive to what she'd been through. He was trying to get her interested in her fate.

"True, but those people are in a state which they do not recover from usually. The Infected killed mercilessly in a blind fit, but once they were administered their Z-shot, they no longer felt that fit of rage that drove them to kill. Whatever made them do what they did was no longer a factor. They were brought back to their right mind."

Doctor Fullerton nodded his head as he considered this. He wrote something down and then turned back to Zooey.

"So the Undead should be absolved of their sins, per say?"

She let out a breathy laugh and pushed her knotted hair behind her shoulders. "I think they should be given a second chance. They didn't ask for this infection. They were simply unfortunate enough to come in contact with it and now that there's a way to control it, I think they should be able to go back to their lives. If they kill again, then yes they deserve punishment just like every other human being, but we shouldn't punish them for being ill."

"Would you feel this way if you yourself weren't infected?"

The muscles in her face fell as she thought. Her eyes stared ahead at the desk vacantly. "I think so, yes," she said, and then changed the subject. "Do you think your wife is still out there, a zombie wandering around, waiting to be found?"

Doctor Fullerton stared at her, his eyes wide and glossy. The pen was poised in his hand as if he forgot what he intended to write. "How do you—"

"There's been speculation," she recovered quickly, adjusting in her seat. "I was just curious why you chose to work with the Undead. You seem to be the only one here who really cares about what happens to us."

"That's not true," he argued. "Each and every person here wants to see you all go out and…" He trailed off when he saw the disbelieving look in her eyes. He sighed. "It's just another reason you should take advantage of your time here. Things have changed since the cure was discovered. Some people are against it. It might be something you have to deal with for the rest of your life…the prejudice, I mean."

Zooey knew the minute she woke up that her life would never be the same as it'd once been. This wasn't news to her. Blood diseases had always been taboo, scaring people out of their minds and making them do crazy and hurtful things in order to protect themselves from it. Zooey was no longer a drooling, growling, viscious zombie, but she still carried it inside her. She could pass it on to someone else without meaning to. That was the thought that scared her the most, more than what she did while she was out there.

"I can handle it," she lied. "I never really cared what people said about me before. Why start now?" She laughed it off.

The corners of the doctor's lips gave a quick tug upward and he wrote some more in the file.

"But the question still stands about your wife."

He froze, his eyes looking up from his work to meet hers. It wasn't anger that burned behind them, more like the desire to know the answer to her question himself.

"I don't know what happened to her," he said, his voice thick with defeat.

"She left you with the kids?"

"We never had children. She couldn't. It was one of the reasons I loved being a family physician so much. I enjoyed being around what I couldn't have myself, but I never wanted her to think I regretted the fact that she couldn't have any."

The doctor opened up as if no one had ever asked him about himself before. Zooey sensed the weight that sat heavy on his shoulders, the worry that lurked inside his mind every waking moment. But why open up to her? She couldn't be sure. She had a caring, quiet side to her that made her an excellent listener, or maybe by telling her something personal about himself, he hoped she would reciprocate. Either way, she listened intently, leaning further forward in her seat.

"We were walking home together through the park one night when...we were attacked. He grabbed her so quickly I didn't have time to react. Before I knew what happened, he had bitten her."

Zooey's eyes watered as she watched the doctor tear-up. "I'm so sorry," she offered.

He sniffed and turned back to his papers. "That was two years ago, right at the beginning of everything, so no, I don't expect her to come through those doors. She's long gone by now, even if she is out there somewhere."

Whoever Ren heard the doctor's story from, they'd gotten it all wrong. Doctor Fullerton wasn't pining for his wife to return to him. He was grieving, trying to accept the fact that he'd never see her again, maybe even living with the fear that he would lay eyes on her shambling body someday, knowing it wasn't his wife anymore.

Zooey tried not to think what it would be like to be stuck as a zombie for two whole years. The two months she was out there was more than she could handle. *More than you could handle now*, a voice in her head spoke to her. It was her own. *But when you were out there, eating the tender juicy morsels of fresh brains...it was all you ever needed in life! It was bliss, and you'll never feel that way again.*

The doctor must have seen something in her eyes, because he leaned forward with his brow furrowed and lips pursed. "Are you feeling okay?" he asked.

Zooey snapped out of it with a quick shake of her head. Before she could answer, a loud scream echoed from down the hallway. Doctor Fullerton raced to the door and peeked his head out.

Two large security officers had Sam Kyle hooked under each arm and were dragging him down the hall. The curly-haired, defiant kid flailed his legs through the air in an attempt to escape, but they had him locked in.

"Let me go, you bastards! Don't take me there! Don't do this!" His voice was deeply seeded with anger, but the closer he drew to the doors the more he changed his tune. "I swear, I'll stop saying things, just please! I don't remember! I DON'T REMEMBER ANYTHING! PLEASE!"

Nurses, doctors, and patients all stood in the hall to watch as Sam Kyle disappeared through the black double doors.

Chapter Seven

Zooey counted the hours, minutes, and seconds of the week until the day until visitors finally arrived. Time moved differently in the Ward. Maybe it was because there were no windows to the outside, no sunlight to show them time really was still moving along. Or maybe it was because with each ridiculous group session time dragged forward like a slug.

Day in and day out, the medical staff at the Massachusetts's General Hospital Undead Ward went through their daily routines of shuffling their patients from one mind-numbing activity to the next. As if Zooey didn't already know there was a fat chance her job would take her back due to her two month sabbatical where she ate people's brains, they also felt it necessary to spend time forming a class to inform her that people might treat her differently, look at her differently, and possibly throw stones at her in the square. (Well, that last part she made up, but it seemed to be where they were headed with it.)

If Zooey had to reenact one more daily interactions with "normal humans", and be gently reminded to use the phrase "It's an Undead thing", to explain her condition, she would scream. When she found herself wanting to beat her head against a wall, she let her mind drift back to Sam Kyle and how he was dragged away, never to be seen again.

The echoes of his voice screaming out that he didn't remember haunted her when things were quiet. Ren was right. They really did want to quiet the ones that remembered. But why? Did they think it would be too difficult to fix if they could see in their minds what they'd done? Every night since she woke up from her zombie-state, Zooey dreamt of the horrors she inflicted on others. She wasn't screaming out at the top of her lungs twenty-four-seven, or trying to hurt herself or others, but she was simply dealing with it, as all the others seemed to be. There was no need for the staff to drag the Undead away, scarring the rest.

As the days went on, eyes grew darker, and shoulders heavier from the weight of guilt. They didn't have to tell anyone that they remembered. Zooey could see it in their faces, hear it in their voices and also in their cries at night. Though her hair was now untangled and shiny, her face healed and the stitches taken out, and her skin had regained some warmth to its color again, Zooey felt worse off than before. The faces of the people she murdered flashed randomly in her mind, jarring her from her reality. The only thing she could do was make light of being Undead and suffer alone inside her heart. If she didn't, then she might be the next one to go through the double doors.

"Everyone make it through the night?" Ren asked Zooey while they waited in line to have their vitals checked, as they did every morning.

"I think so," She said.

She looked over her shoulder to see who was still shuffling out of their rooms, rubbing their eyes and stretching their arms over their heads.

"What a way to go," he said shaking his head. "They find a way to bring us back to life, only to drag us through those doors and kill us again. It's inhumane."

"You don't actually think they're killing them, do you?" It was what Zooey feared since Sam disappeared. She never liked the kid, with his unkempt, overgrown hair and stoner eyes that drooped with disinterest, but she never wanted him dead.

"What else could they be doing with them? Why hasn't Sam come back to the group yet? It's been almost a week."

Zooey shrugged her shoulders and stared ahead at Shelly Johnson's wavy blonde mom-bob.

Normally, the woman would be biting her nails and cursing the staff for not letting her call her family, but today was different. Everyone was in a better mood, their spirits lightened, because it was the first day of visitation.

Doctor Fullerton assured Zooey in their last session that both Elizabeth and Oliver confirmed they were coming to see her, something the other two resident doctors hadn't bothered doing for their own patients. They would be allowed an entire fifteen minutes with their guests with only bulletproof glass separating them. Zooey wasn't even sure she'd have enough to say to fill the time. There was so much she wasn't allowed to talk about.

"Got anyone coming to see you?" she asked Ren in an attempt to change the subject.

He shook his head. "I'm originally from Chicago so no family here…not that I have any there either."

"And you still can't remember your last name?" Zooey asked, as she did almost every day.

He shook his head again and averted his eyes to scan the room.

"That's so strange. I remember everything about my life before."

"Must be different for everyone. You know how medical stuff is. Totally unpredictable."

"I guess," she said. "On another note, your beard is coming along nicely."

She forced a smile as she stared up at him. Something she used to do so freely before felt wrong now, like a simple grin.

He ran his fingers through his stubble. His eyes beamed. "Ya think? I just wanted to cover up the scars as best I could. Lucky they're all on my chin, really."

There was nothing Zooey could do to hide the angry marks on her face. They were there for the whole world to see and judge. She disappeared into self-pity, not noticing as Ren leaned closer into her.

"So, you remember anything else?" he whispered in her ear.

Her eyes narrowed as she thought about how to approach his question. He was, after all, like her. She looked into his soft, gray eyes and decided she was being paranoid.

"Every night it's a different one."

He nodded his head sympathetically. "Me too."

"It's awful, isn't it? I almost can't bear it."

"Yeah," he said absently, as if he were thinking of something else. "Yeah, it's rough, but it is nice to feel that brain high again, even if it is only in a dream."

She whipped her head to glare up at him.

He smiled down at her. "That brain high. That indescribable feeling of bliss, power, and pleasure unlike anything else in this world. You remember what it was like, don't you?"

Zooey shook her head and stared forward again. She thought she was the only one who felt that incredible feeling when she dreamed of slurping the brain-matter from someone's skull. It wasn't something she allowed herself to think about for too long. If she did, she ended up craving that feeling and the brains supplied it. She didn't dare tell Ren this, or anyone else. That was something the world didn't want to know about the Undead.

Zooey stood at the front of the line. The same nurse who'd given her the most horrific sponge-bath in history stuck her head out and called for the next person. Their eyes locked before the nurse disappeared into the room. She'd looked at Zooey as if they'd never met. Zooey blinked in disbelief until the nurse called out for her again gruffly.

After she checked Zooey's temperature and blood pressure, not without a few slurs grumbled under her breath, she released Zooey back to her room to freshen up before visitation.

As Zooey looked at herself in the grimy bathroom mirror, she wished they could have scrounged up some clothes for them to wear so she didn't have to go out there looking like a mental patient, but maybe it was fitting. She didn't feel her best mentally. In fact, the longer she stayed in the Ward, the more unsure she felt about her place in the world. Seeing her two best friends couldn't have come at a better time.

She heard the shuffling of feet as she sat on the bed running a plastic comb through her long, brown hair. Nurse Shawn had someone by the arm and was helping them down the hall. It wasn't anyone Zooey had seen before. The woman had thin, scraggly hair with chunks missing here and there. Her face was swollen twice its normal size on the right and the left was so badly scratched she could barely make out what was what. The woman moaned with each step she took.

Zooey held her breath as she reminded herself that things could be worse than a few scratches and a new life. Not only could she be mauled beyond recognition like the woman struggling to make it to Alissa's old bed, but she could still be out there like countless others were. She could be beyond help and executed on the spot instead of brought here to recover.

And I could be eating brains right now, flying higher and higher until I'm on top of the world.

Zooey stopped brushing and stared at the blank wall in front of her.

"Shut up, shut up, shut up," she said just loud enough for her to hear.

Chapter Eight

Zooey walked in a single-file line with the rest of the patients down a long stretch of hallway. There was a distinct bounce in her step as she trotted along. Her hand kept reaching up to smooth out her hair. She was about to see her friends for the first time since she disappeared two months ago.

The patients were led by an unfamiliar male nurse with spikey white-blond hair and tattoos down both arms. The same security officer that led Zooey to her sponge bath only five days ago moved behind the wiry nurse in a hulking manner to a small door with a window. Zooey craned her neck to get a glimpse inside, but it was impossible to see around David Stern's wide frame and large head. The nurse held a clipboard in his hands firmly and positioned himself on one side of the door while the security officer guarded from the other side. His rippling arms folded over his broad chest menacingly, but his kind, brown eyes smiled.

"Tamara Knox!" the nurse called out.

The woman gave a loud whoop that echoed down the empty hall as she pushed her way to the front. "I knew my man would come!" She disappeared through the door with a smile that wrinkled the array of scars on her face.

"Derek Lawson!"

The twenty-year-old boy moved to the front of the line, his large curls bouncing with each step. His hands fidgeted at his sides as he stared at the door. With a deep breath, he opened it and went in.

"David Stern!"

The large man already in the front and laughed aloud after a loud clap of his hands. "See you all in there!" he said in his booming voice. He disappeared behind the door.

Zooey's stomach sank from the possibility that Elizabeth and Oliver had changed their minds once they were briefed on her condition and all the horror she wreaked as a zombie. Maybe they didn't want an Undead as their friend. Maybe everything Zooey did as a zombie, everything that she now remembered clearly, was too much for them to forgive and forget.

"Zooey Beckett!"

She exhaled an audible sigh of relief and made for the door.

"Everyone else, you can follow me back to the common room for free time."

Shelly Johnson rushed to the front and almost knocked Zooey out of the way to get to the door. "No!" she cried hysterically. "My family's in there. My kids are waiting for me!"

The nurse rolled his eyes and gave a deep huff before signaling to the security officer, who wrapped his arms around Shelly's waist and lifted her up. The woman kicked her legs out as she grunted and growled.

"NO! I HAVE TO SEE MY FAMILY!"

"You're family isn't here," the nurse tried to tell her, but she was too far gone to hear him.

Tears streamed down her cheeks as she thrashed about wildly.

Zooey looked on in horror. Her heart ached for the woman. All she'd talked about for the last week was seeing her family again. She couldn't help wondering why they weren't there—did they no longer want her in the family, or did she eat them? The thought should have sickened Zooey more than it did, but she'd thought worse things since being back.

As Shelly's cries drifted further down the hall, Zooey turned to the door and took a breath. She peered through the tiny window. Elizabeth and Oliver were sitting next to each other. In the center of the large room was a long table that ran the entire length with thick glass separating the sides. Every few feet there were dividers for privacy. *Like prison,* Zooey thought, but she'd long since realized the Undead were not treated with much care or respect. She wasn't surprised at all to see how dank, dark, and uninviting the place was.

Elizabeth sat with her arms folded across her chest. Occasionally, she would tug at her tan blazer and shift in her seat. Her back hovered in front of the metal folding chair as she sat rigid.

Oliver, on the other hand, leaned back with his hands behind his head and a smile on his face. He wore a black t-shirt that made his bright orange hair stand out like it was on fire. It was shagged up as if he'd just rolled out of bed and ran his fingers through it moments ago.

Zooey smiled as she felt warmth spread through her chest. She went through the door, unable to contain the joy that wanted to pour out of her.

But as soon as Elizabeth's eyes fell on her, they were overtaken with tears. Her bottom lip quivered as Zooey sat down.

"Oh my god," she said with a shaky voice. "I can't believe you're actually here. We thought you were—"

"It's good to see you," Oliver interrupted, now leaning forward in his seat, the smile gone from his lips.

"I'm so glad to see you guys too. This has been the longest week of my life."

Elizabeth sniffed and flicked the wetness from under her eyes. She tried to pull herself together by clearing her throat. "Are you all right? Your face…and you've lost so much weight."

"I know, it's weird. All I've been doing the last two months is eating." A tiny smile played at her lips.

Oliver snorted with laughter. Elizabeth gave him a sharp look and nudged him with her elbow.

"It's not funny!" She turned to Zooey. "It's not funny, Zoe. Don't joke about that."

Zooey shrugged her shoulders and rested her elbows on the table. "It's the only way to get through it all really."

Elizabeth's eyes started to water again. "When you never came home, I thought you were dead. This one went out every single day looking for you because the damn police wouldn't lift a finger to help."

Zooey's eyes fell on Oliver, whose cheeks were burning red. He shifted in his chair and rubbed his hands together.

"Yeah, well, it's no big deal."

She gazed into his green eyes, swallowing the lump that formed in her throat. "It is a big deal. You could have gotten hurt, or bit. Thank you." She tried her best to impregnate her gratitude into her every single word that stumbled from her lips.

His eyes softened on her for just a moment, and then he rubbed at the back of his neck, a soft smile taking over his warm face.

Elizabeth was still trying to fight back the tears that wanted to spill from her eyes. It pained Zooey to see the misery she caused her dearest friend.

"Why don't we talk about something else?" Zooey turned to Oliver. "How's the music thing going?"

He perked up in his seat right away. "It's actually going really well. No matter what state the world is in, people will always drink and when they're drunk they'll listen to anything. That's where I come in."

"And what do you do exactly?" Elizabeth asked him for the twentieth time that year, her signature bite working its way back into her voice.

"He's a bluesy, indie-pop solo artist," Zooey answered.

"Who occasionally hires a band to round out his sound," Oliver added.

"Really? Since when?"

"Just a few weeks ago. I found these guys that are really awesome for my sound. It makes a huge difference in some of my more upbeat songs when an acoustic guitar just isn't—"

"School is starting back up," Elizabeth cut in with an eye roll.

Zooey's eyes widened and she perked up in her seat. "It is? When?"

"The end of August, about a week after you're supposed to be released from this place." She looked around the room as if she were seeing it for the first time, her nose wrinkled in disgust, and then turned back to her friend. "I could bring you the paperwork to fill out and hand it in for you if you like."

"For what?"

"To go back to school, of course."

Zooey hadn't thought about going back to school. It hadn't come up in one of their infamous role-playing sessions yet. Honestly, besides going back to her apartment, she didn't know what she was going to do with her Undead life.

"I haven't decided if I want to—"

"Stop right there," Elizabeth said with her hand raised. "If you think you're going to come back just to mope around, start wearing all back, and cut off all your hair, you're wrong. I won't let you. Yes, something truly awful and horrifying happened to you and it's going to take time to recover. We don't expect you to be your old self in a day."

"I do, but I have really high standards."

"Shut up, Oliver!" Elizabeth hissed with narrowed eyes. "We know this will be an...adjustment.

But the worst thing you could do is pull yourself away from everyone and everything you love." She looked at her Undead friend with an intensity that burned behind her large brown eyes.

Zooey had to look down at her lap to avoid getting scorched by her gaze.

"You love helping people. That's why you wanted to study psychology in the first place, remember? You can't give up because of a little setback that—"

It was Zooey's turn to interrupt. "A little setback? You have no idea what I've been through these last two months, what I've seen, what I've done!"

"Wait, are you saying you remember?" Oliver leaned forward to ask.

His voice carried louder than Zooey would have liked. She frantically looked around to see if anyone had heard. The security guard and nurse stood by the door still and were deep in conversation about which motorcycle was cooler—a Harley or a Ducati. She let out the tension in her shoulders and turned back to her friends.

"I can just...I can imagine is all," she recovered quickly.

Elizabeth scrutinized her friend, eyeing her carefully to find some crack in her composed façade that would reveal what was really going on inside her

Undead head. But Zooey was determined to keep it all a secret. She wasn't ready to let anyone know the details of her time as a zombie.

Elizabeth was a perceptive person. She changed the subject. "I tried to convince this one to come back too, but he won't," she forced a breathy laugh as she nudged Oliver in the ribs again.

"No way!" he cracked a smile and wriggled away from her jabbing elbow. "I hated it there."

"No one hates Harvard," she retorted.

"I did! All the Dockers and dorky haircuts. No thanks."

Elizabeth rolled her eyes. "You were one semester away from getting your degree. If the world hadn't gone to shit and you hadn't quit, you could be a lawyer right now."

Oliver wrinkled his nose and glared at her.

"Whatever. I'm done trying to help you. Get another ridiculous tattoo and keep strumming your guitar for quarters if it makes you happy."

He nodded with a satisfied smile and leaned back with his hands behind his head again. "It does, thank you."

Tears had collected in the corners of Zooey's eyes as she quietly watched her friends bicker.

"Sweetie, what is it?" Elizabeth shot forward so fast she almost hit her head on the glass. "Does something hurt? Should we ask for help?"

Zooey shook her head as the tears fell. She brushed them away, feeling her ears burn under her hair. "No, I'm fine...it's just...I really missed you guys."

Oliver wiped at his mouth with both hands and then leaned forward to rest his elbows on his knees. The only part of his face visible were his moist, brilliant eyes.

"We missed you too," Elizabeth spoke for the both of them, putting her hand on Oliver's back.

"Two minutes!" one of the security guards shouted across the room.

Zooey whipped around in her seat to look at him as if he were lying. There was no way they had been sitting there for thirteen minutes already. It only felt like five. Suddenly, her chest tightened. She struggled to take in a breath. In two minutes Elizabeth and Oliver would return to the real world and she would be ushered back into Undead Hell.

"Before you go, can you do something for me?" she turned back to the pair and asked softly.

"Of course, anything," Elizabeth answered.

"No, Oliver..."

He raised his head, wide-eyed, as if he'd been called on in class. His hands ran over his ginger hair. "Sure, what is it?" he said.

"Do you think you could sing for me? Just a few lines or something. It's just…I'm really starting to freak out about going back in there for another two weeks and whenever I had trouble falling asleep at the apartment I would listen to you singing through the walls while you were writing new songs and it…I don't know…it relaxed me."

He nodded his head and readjusted himself in his chair to sit upright. His fingers flexed around his knees and then relaxed as he closed his eyes

"You said you'd be home not a minute too late,
I said don't worry, there's no need to hurry,
But you never made it back, I guess it was simply your
fate, and I, I can't help wo-o-o-ndering—"

He sand out in a voice that was somehow soft with emotion and strong with confidence as the same time.

Zooey sat back and watched through misty eyes as his Atom's apple worked up and down to push out the voice that had danced her to sleep for the last three years.

"Hey, you! Knock it off!" the security officer shouted, pointing a sausage-like finger at Oliver while the nurse scowled.

He smiled, red-faced, and laughed.

Zooey smiled back, tears still stinging in her eyes. "That was perfect."

Chapter Nine

Cold, stiff hands dug into the abdomen of the man lying on the ground. Blood poured out from him and onto the green grass. Zooey held up one of her hands, letting the moonlight shine down on its slick red coating. She studied it, mesmerized…and then she lunged forward, burying her face in the carnage.

"I WON'T TAKE IT!"

Zooey's eyes popped open. Her chest heaved heavily as she lie on her back. Sweat drenched her thin clothes and sheets. She looked over and saw that Chastity was still sound asleep, curled up in a ball like a kitten.

"I won't take that shit!" She thought the voice was part of her dream. "Who knows what it really is!" it rang out again.

"Mr. Tat, you need to take your Z-shot early. It isn't lasting as long in your system as it does with the younger Undead."

"What a load of bullshit," the old man grumbled. "You say it's my shot, but who knows what's really in there. You could be doping me up to steal my organs for all I know!"

Zooey quickly got out of bed and went to her door. She peered through the crack to see Nurse Shawn with the night security officer, an average man in every way, standing in the hallway near the desk facing an irritated Benjamin Tat.

"Ben, we're in a hospital, not some back alley," Shawn huffed.

"Don't call me Ben with that disrespectful tone, young man. I said I won't take it and that's that! I never asked for you to cure me! I never wanted any of this!"

Shawn looked to the security officer and gave a single nod. As Benjamin was going on about how he would have been just as happy to wander the airport as a zombie for the rest of his short life, the completely ordinary man aimed his gun at the old man's head and fired.

The blast knocked Zooey off her feet. She fell back into the room and scrambled away on her hands and feet. When her spine touched the wall, she curled her feet up under her and rocked back and forth, biting her nails.

Chastity sat up, slightly swaying with sleepiness. "What was that?"

Zooey pushed herself up, gripping the wall, and covered her mouth with her hands, unable to say a word.

"What was that?" her roommate repeated more urgently.

Chastity got out of bed and headed for the door. Zooey wanted to stop her. She had no idea what the rules were anymore. Her heart raced as she thought of them opening fire on the young girl.

Her roommate disappeared into the dimly lit hall. Zooey finally regained the feeling in her legs and ran to the door just in time to see the two men dragging Benjamin Tat's body through the black double doors. Several others wandered out of their rooms to see what the commotion was about. A small pool of blood crept outward on the white tile floor.

"My God," Chastity mumbled as she placed a hand over her parted lips.

Shelly Johnson pointed at the puddle, her mouth open as if she were about to have another outburst, but she quickly snapped it shut and lowered her hand. Derek Lawson tugged at his thick hair nervously while David leaned against their doorframe. Zooey spotted Ren, who locked eyes with her.

At breakfast everyone went about their business as if nothing happened. No one asked questions, and Zooey figured that was just how the staff wanted it.

"I'm just counting the minutes till we get out of here, Zooey girl," Ren said with a mouthful of watered-down scrambled eggs. "You never know who's going to disappear next."

His eyes had large, dark circles under them. The soft skin was puffy from a lack of sleep. Every so often he would glance to his left and then right as if expecting someone to come up and grab him. Everyone else at the breakfast table sat hunched over, tense and shifty-eyed as if cruel death were closing in on them.

"I saw it and I still don't really understand," Zooey said flatly as she stared at her untouched food. "He was being difficult about taking his medication, but that was all. They could have easily gotten a few guys to hold him down and given it to him."

"Ah, but isn't it so much easier to just eliminate any Undead who shows the slightest signs of resistance?"

Zooey turned to look at Ren, his dark hair ruffled and wild.

His eyes roamed the room. She realized he wasn't nervous about being taken next, he was checking to make sure none of the staff was able to hear what he said.

"The man wasn't entirely wrong, though, you know?"

Zooey's brow pulled together as her eyes narrowed. She cocked her head to the side. "What do you mean?"

"I mean none of us asked to be 'saved'," he said bitterly, his fingers raised in air quotes. He turned in his seat toward her. Their knees touched lightly. "Tell me, if they hadn't scooped you up and given you your Z-shot, how would you feel?"

Zooey stared back blankly. As a zombie, she wandered around never feeling an ounce of pain—no sadness, no anxiousness, no guilt, no anger—none of those inconvenient feelings everyone else was burdened with. All she felt was an incomprehensible amount of bliss and the desire to feel it again once it inevitably faded.

Ren stared at her eagerly with his eyebrows raised, urging the truth from her.

"I guess I would feel what we all felt…happy."

He clapped his hands together loudly as he scooted back and smiled with all his teeth. "Yes! There it is! That's what I'm talking about!"

Zooey looked around and noticed some of the others were staring. Ren had always been one of the stranger ones in the bunch, so the fact that the others were looking at him and shaking their heads didn't faze him in the least. Zooey, on the other hand, hung her head so her hair hid her burning cheeks. Being the center of attention was the last thing she wanted, especially in the Undead Ward. She didn't want to be known for being Ren the rebel's friend.

"Nobody wants to be a zombie," she answered matter-of-factly.

"If they've never been one."

She turned back to her food and stabbed at it with her spork, hoping he would take the hint and stop talking. He did, but his smile never faded.

That afternoon Zooey went to her daily session with Doctor Fullerton.

"How are things, considering," he said, his voice dripping with remorse.

She shrugged her shoulders, not really wanting to talk about another Undead being killed.

"If I had a nickel for every time you answered one of my questions with a shrug I'd be a very rich man," he said in a fatherly tone as he tried to conceal a grin. "How was your visit with your friends?"

Her head turned upward. In all the craziness, she had almost forgotten about her extremely short visit with Elizabeth and Oliver.

"It was good," was all she offered.

Doctor Fullerton wrote on his notepad for a minute. He then took off his wire-rimmed glasses and put them in his breast pocket. His soft eyes stared in silence until she couldn't take it, a trick they had taught her in school when dealing with a patient who won't open up.

"What did you talk about with them?"

Zooey sighed. He wasn't going to give up until she gave him something. "What they've been up to, what it's like here, me coming home, school…"

"Are you going back to school?"

She stared forward in thought. "If they'll take me," she said self-deprecatingly.

"You know, there are laws to protect the Undead now, help them to start over again. One of those laws is that a school cannot deny an Undead placement if they qualify. There are even special scholarship programs to help them…you…further your education."

Zooey nodded her head as if she were taking in every word the good doctor said, but really she was trying to picture her life if she went back to school—people staring, whispering behind her back, everyone avoiding her because of what she had done. Then, she tried to picture her life if she didn't go back—living in a tiny apartment, eventually alone because Elizabeth was set to marry Kenneth soon and move out. She would work some minimum wage job just to survive and probably end up drinking herself to death.

"Yeah, I think I do want to go back."

"Excellent!" Doctor Fullerton said with a wide grin. "I think that's a great idea."

"And maybe when I get my degree I can open my own practice and counsel the Undead, help them through everything."

At first the doctor's eyes lit up, but slowly they grew dim as his face froze and then relaxed back into a melodramatic stare. "Why would you want to do that?"

Zooey narrowed her eyes disbelievingly. It seemed like the only plan that made any sense. She was Undead, so why not help others going through what she herself had already dealt with?

"I want to help."

"You could always volunteer at the Ward. We could always use helping hands."

The thought of spending another minute there made her nose wrinkle. "No offense, but I don't plan on coming back here once I'm released."

"You don't like it here?" He asked the question as if he didn't know the answer, but the way his eyes glistened told her he knew very well no one wanted to be there…not even him.

"I just think there will be a lot of Undead who still need someone to talk to once they are released and no offense to you, but they might be more willing to open up about their experiences with someone who is like them, who went through the same things they did."

"What experiences would they have to open up about if they can't remember being a zombie, as you say you can't?"

Zooey stared ahead. How did she get herself trapped like this? Why did it always come back to if she remembered or not? She was starting to think that was the only reason the hospital kept them so long. They wanted to weed out the ones who might remember the things they'd done. But why? With the right help, they could move past it all and start to build a normal life again. At least, that was what Zooey hoped.

Later that evening during free time, Zooey told Ren about the doctor's disapproval of her wanting to counsel the Undead.

Ren huffed out a breath of air. "He just doesn't want a place for the Undead to gather together. He thinks if they come to you instead of him, they'll tell you all the things they remember and then they'll never get a chance to eliminate them like they did Sam Kyle or Benjamin Tat."

Zooey considered this. Was the world really that scared of them? They had no reason to be. Undead were just regular people, so long as they took their medication. What was there to fear from them getting psychological help if they needed it?

"They're afraid that if we have somewhere to rally and talk about our feelings that we'll form some kind of rebellion for being treated like second-class citizens."

Ren was always going on about conspiracy theories. Zooey couldn't help wondering if he was like that before he became an Undead, or if it was a new development. Surely, he couldn't have always been so paranoid, but then again, she knew nothing about him and his former life.

"I don't know," she deflected. "Anyway, I guess I'm just going to go back to school for my Masters in Psychology and see where it takes me. Who knows if I'll even be able to find work being what I am now."

"So true, darling. No one knows. Things change daily out there."

Zooey's bottom lip tucked in. She was someone who liked order, rules, a set schedule. Now that her life was tossed into the air with no real direction, her chest felt constantly constricted. What kind of life would be waiting for her once she was released? None of the Undead seemed to have a clue, even the ones who had families to go back to weren't sure if they'd be there when they got out.

"One thing that doesn't change, though, is brains," Ren said with a distant look in his eyes.

Zooey turned to him with her brow knit tightly together. "What did you say?" she asked sharply.

"Brains," he said casually. "No matter how many Z-shots they give us, the desire for brains never really goes away, does it? It only subsides momentarily to get us through the next few days."

Zooey hated to admit it, but he was right. She was only days away from getting her second shot, and with each passing hour she was less sure she would make it. No matter who she looked at, the first thing that popped into her head was their brain—how big it was, what it tasted like, what it would make her feel if she devoured it. Each and every brain was different, bringing about its own unique and euphoric high. Her body ached to feel it again.

Ren looked at her with his head tilted to one side, his eyes trying to penetrate her own brain and see what was going on inside.

Chapter Ten

What was left of the group gathered in the common area to do another round of roleplaying.

"Some of you will be employees at a retail clothing store while the other half acts as customers needing help. Let's do this for about fifteen minutes and then we'll switch roles. Break off into pairs and begin," Nurse Devin said, his voice breaking halfway through.

It was his first time running a group session without Nurse Shawn. The Undead looked at him with large, unblinking eyes as he read word-for-word from his clipboard. Every so often, his thin eyes would dart up, catch a glimpse of them staring at him, and look back down nervously. He cleared his throat.

Zooey wasn't sure if it was the fact that they were a group of former zombies and he was the only human in the room who hadn't died before, or if he was nervous for his job. It was a fleeting wonder, quickly dispersing from a lack of care. She couldn't bring herself to care about anything anymore. The Ward was becoming unbearable with each passing second. If she didn't get her Z-shot soon she was going to jump on poor, little Devin like a lion, crack his skull open, and drink from it. These thoughts plagued her every waking minute the past few days.

"Want to be my partner?" Ren asked as he rammed his shoulder into hers playfully.

Zooey turned to him, stone-faced, and shrugged her shoulders. "Sure. Why not? Not like we have a choice in the matter."

"What's got your panties in a bunch this morning?" A smile tugged at his lips.

He waited for a response, but Zooey didn't give him one. She was done being nice and done playing by the rules. She wanted her shot and to get the hell out of there already. Her knuckles cracked continuously as she fidgeted with her hands.

Brains—brains—BRAINS!

She couldn't turn the voice off in her head. It shouted at her day and night, growing louder as she waited. Clearly, two weeks was too long to go between shots. She wanted to tell this to Doctor Fullerton, but she was still on the fence about him. At times he seemed to sympathize, like when he read her their rights regarding school, and then other times he seemed to be as narrow-minded and judgmental as everyone else there, like when he was discouraging her from helping the Undead. She was worried if she told him they needed Z-shots more frequently he would nod his head and someone would pop out from behind the door and shoot her.

God, I sounds like Ren, she would think to herself whenever she had these thoughts. Maybe he was right to be so paranoid, though. It had kept him alive this long. The same couldn't be said about young Sam Kyle or old man Tat. But if she murdered the stuttering nurse in front of everyone, someone would surely shoot her.

"Do you want to be the employee?" Ren asked, pulling her from her stupor.

"Sure," she said disinterested.

He jumped right in with a horrible British accent. "Hello, Miss. I'm looking for a pair of rainbow colored suspenders, but it seems you only have them in tri-color." He gave Zooey a smile, expecting one in return.

Her face was blank and unmoving, her eyes dull and lifeless. She gave him nothing.

"Say, Miss, hope you don't mind me asking, but what's with the scars on your face there?"

The accent was getting ridiculous. She had to work hard not to crack a smile. Ren saw this and pushed forward.

"Did you get hit by a trolley on your way to the local pub for some fish-n-chips?"

He lifted his thick eyebrows, egging her on.

Zooey huffed through her nostrils and looked up at the ceiling.

"Go on, Zooey girl, say it," he said in a sing-song manner.

"It's so stupid."

He stared at her, waiting.

"Nothing to worry about, Sir," she said as flat as her voice could carry. "It's…" She sighed. "It's an Undead thing."

Ren clapped his hands together. "Bravo! Award-winning performance from the great Zooey Marie Beckett. She'll be here all week, ladies and gentlemen."

"Don't remind me," she grumbled.

He put his arm around her shoulder and reeled her into him. "Oh, come on. It's not all that bad, is it?"

She looked up at him challengingly.

"You have me at least!"

Wriggling out of his grasp, she said, "At least there's that."

She really did like Ren. Whenever they were thrown together for one of their ridiculous group sessions, he always found a way to make her laugh and take her mind off the thoughts that were trying to claw their way through her head. But it was the other moments, the ones where he would casually reminisce about eating brains and the feeling it gave him (and her) that made her keep him at arms' length. She would often feel guilty for this. How could she blame him when the same thoughts were going through her mind?

"I can't believe they're making us say this garbage. It's ridiculous. Why would any of us in our right mind ever say anything is an Undead thing? It's like they want to keep us forever separated from the general public."

Zooey dove headfirst into a rant. She couldn't stop herself. Everything she felt for the last two weeks came bubbling up to the surface until it spilled out of her mouth like the bile that used to trickle down her chin.

Ren looked at her wide-eyed, and then to a spot over her shoulder. Terror crept into his dark irises.

"They don't want us to reintegrate ourselves back into our old lives! They want to put us in our place and keep us there because they think we're the scum of the earth and—"

"Problem, Miss Beckett?" a squeaky voice asked from behind.

She could tell Devin was trying to assert himself, prove that he could be left in charge once in a while just to get out from under giant Shawn's thumb, but Zooey was in no mood. She'd had enough and it was time she told someone off about it.

"Yeah I have a—"

Out of nowhere, Ren socked poor, young Devin in the mouth. The nurse fell to the floor, clutching at his face as tears collected in his soft eyes.

"Undeads rule!" Ren shouted like a maniac, his hands raised over his head triumphantly.

Two security officers raced out of their tiny office in the corner and seized him by each arm.

"Ren!" Zooey shouted, trying to reach out to him.

They dragged him away from the group and down the hall. As he disappeared through the black double doors, Zooey caught one last glimpse of his playful smile.

The room fell silent.

Ren was gone.

Chapter Eleven

Zooey tossed and turned in her twin-size bed that night. She couldn't get the image of Ren being dragged through those doors out of her head. If he had been right about what they did back there, then there was no chance of ever seeing him again. When he was at her side, laying out his conspiracy theories to her, she often wished he would go away. Now that he was gone, she'd give anything to have him back. It wasn't until now that she realized he was her only true Undead friend, the only other person she could talk to about what she was going through.

On a normal day, in her normal apartment, the orange rays of the rising sun would creep through the blinds and gently wake her up. She would stretch her arms, sigh, smile, and get out of bed with a positive attitude that could tackle any challenge of the day. But in the Undead Ward, her room went from pitch black to blindingly light in a single second as the morning wake-up nurse did her rounds.

"Get up!" she hollered into the room as she flipped on the switch to the fluorescent lighting.

Zooey threw an arm over her face to hide her eyes. She wanted to crawl under the blankets until it was her time to leave. She was beginning to think that was the only way she'd get out of there alive.

"Z-shots today!" the woman hollered down the hall.

There wasn't anything she could have said to get the Undead moving quicker. Each and every one stumbled out of their rooms eagerly, tying their thin robes around their waist, bare-footed and stumbling on stiff legs. Zooey got in line as quick as she could. She wanted nothing more than to turn off the voice in her head and feel human again, if only for a week.

Her desire for brains had become overwhelming in the last twenty-four hours. She could see it in the dreary eyes of the others too. Every thought she had ultimately came back around to shoving brains in her mouth, like the seven degrees of Kevin Bacon—Ren led to unknowing, unknowing led to worry, worry led to fear, fear led to death, death led to the jogger she'd smashed open, which led to brains. See! Seven degrees of yummy brains! She gnawed at her lip as the first person was pulled into the tiny office for their morning check-up.

She was so distracted by her attempts at self-discipline to not think about brains that she almost forgot it was the day Oliver and Elizabeth were coming to visit again. Once a week they were allowed outside interaction. It had to be some form of torture—give them just enough and then take it away and see how long until they cracked. Zooey was at her wit's end. Her outburst the other day proved that. If Ren hadn't stepped in like he had, she would have been the one to go through the doors and then God knows what would have happened to her. She felt grateful and guilty for her savior's actions.

"Zooey," Doctor Fullerton's gentle voice called from the doorway. "Zooey, come on in."

She blinked and tucked her thick hair behind her ear, revealing the long scar down her cheek. The stitches had been taken out and all that was left was a purple jagged line. It would be there forever to tell the world what she was.

The doctor sat down and pulled out an enormous needle as long as a pencil and about half as thick. Zooey's stomach clenched tight, her eyes bulging from her head.

"Don't worry, it doesn't hurt too much." He pulled a thick, gel-like liquid up into the syringe and flicked it several times with his index finger. "I'm going to need you to bend over that gurney and hold onto the other side with both your hands. Then, I will lower your trousers a bit to administer the shot, okay?"

He asked, but she knew it wasn't a question. She felt as if her lungs were being squeezed by some medieval torture device, leaving her unable to let a single breath out to replenish. Needles had never bothered her, but she'd never seen one like this before. She swallowed, feeling a hard lump travel down her throat.

Doctor Fullerton gave a pained grin and nodded his head to the gurney. She followed his orders, lowering herself over the surface to grip the other side. With every step he took toward her, the muscles in her neck tightened until they ached.

"Now, just take a deep breath and relax," he said in a slow, soothing voice. "One…two…"

Her entire body clenched in anticipation.

"Three."

The needled forced its way through the soft part of her left buttock. Her first thought was that it hadn't hurt as much as she thought it would. But then he pushed down on the syringe and the Z-shot worked its way through the needle and under her skin. It felt as if he were pushing thick and chunky peanut butter into her. She pulled forward as far as she could go, standing on her tiptoes to get away from the pressure.

"Ow, ow, ow," she whispered through gritted teeth.

"A-a-a-a-and, we're done," he said, pulling the needle out slowly. "You'll want to massage that around so that it doesn't stay clumped up. If it does it gets pretty sore."

"I don't think it could get any worse," she grumbled as she pulled her hospital pants up.

"You'd be surprised." He turned his back to her to prepare another shot for the next patient.

"And I have to get that every two weeks?"

"I'm afraid so."

Zooey rubbed at the aching spot on her butt-cheek. Suddenly, she was glad she only had to sit down for fifteen minutes to talk to her friends. She was sure she, along with everyone else, would be standing around the rest of the day.

"You'll want to stay off your feet as much as possible," the doctor chimed in as she limped to the door. "The more pressure you put on it, the longer it will take for the pain to dissipate."

"Brilliant," she said sarcastically.

She hobbled back to her room to stand over her bed. They weren't allowed to lay down during the day. If they did it was a big flashing sign to the nurses that they were depressed and needed to be hauled through the doors for further treatment. She couldn't sit on the bed because her ass currently felt like it'd been hit with a fifty pound cannonball. If there wasn't a black and purple bruise around the entry point, it would be an Undead miracle. But she wasn't allowed to stand either. Well, she was, but she wasn't sure she could handle any more of the pain that attacked the area.

As she contemplated what to do in the time left before her visit, Chastity walked in holding her backside like an old crone. Tears glistened in her eyes. She sucked in a deep breath with every step she took. For once, Zooey was thankful for the extra layer of fat on her bottom. She couldn't imagine how much it hurt for a stick figure like Chastity to be jabbed with that monstrous needle.

Time went by slowly with Zooey alternating every ten minutes between sitting on the bed and, leaning against the windowsill. She tried to read, but all the books were outdated romance novels donated by lonely old ladies with nothing better to do than fantasize about Fabio. It wasn't until she looked at the clock that she realized she'd gone an entire two hours without thinking about brains. For all the pain it caused, at least the Z-shot was effective and quick.

David Stern and Zooey were the only ones ushered down the long, empty hallway to the visiting area later that day. The normally chatty man walked behind the nurse with a somber face, eyes forward.

Ever since Shelly Johnson's family stood her up, everyone feared the same would happen to them. Just the other day she received a letter. She ripped it open frantically, hoping it was news from her husband, but it was divorce papers from his lawyer.

"In ya go," the security officer held the door open for Zooey. He smiled at her as she passed through.

Her eyes stayed with his, her head turning to look behind her as she moved forward. She finally smiled back, causing the man to grin wider.

Once inside the dingy room, she saw Oliver sitting there with a crooked grin. He was alone.

"Where's Elizabeth?"

"She's running around like a maniac getting school stuff ready for you two, and then Kenneth is taking her out for their fiftieth anniversary or something," he said with a quick roll of his brilliant green eyes.

The blue t-shirt he wore stood out against his fair skin. The colorful tattoos that ran down both his arms seemed to dance as he folded them across his chest and heaved.

"You know, for a guy who spends his days writing mostly love songs you sure are cynical."

Zooey couldn't help cracking a smile when she saw a playful expression flash across his face. He said nothing in his defense.

"And you sure write a lot of love songs for someone who's never been in a relationship longer than three months."

He laughed at this and ran a hand through his orange hair. "I have too! Remember what's her name sophomore year? Kimberly? Katy? Whatever?"

"Your soulmate?"

"We went out for almost five months."

Zooey smiled. "My mistake."

"So, what's been going on in the Ward? Any juicy gossip?"

She leaned back in her seat as she thought about all that'd happened since their last visit. "Ren was taken away," she said softly as she stared at her slippers. "Through the doors."

"That's the guy who was always bothering you?"

"He didn't bother me," she jumped to the defense. "He was my friend."

Oliver raised his hands in surrender. "I come in peace." His voice was light, but his eyes were narrowed and shifty. "So they took him away. What does that mean?"

"I don't know. He hasn't come back. No one comes back once they're taken through the doors. I don't know if he's alive or dead or what they're doing to him. They could have lobotomized him for all I know and it's all my fault."

Oliver leaned so far forward in his chair that his nose almost touched the glass. "What do you mean it's your fault?"

"I was complaining about the roleplaying exercises and was about to throw a fit to the nurse when Ren stepped in and…distracted them…so I wouldn't be punished."

"Jesus, Zoe, don't you know when to keep your mouth shut?"

From anyone else, the words would have fallen flat on her ears. Once Zooey made up her mind about something, there was nothing anyone could say to change it. She had an overzealous need to speak up that no one had ever been able to tame out of her. But hearing that from Oliver stung a bit. She gave a slight wince as he lowered his head into his hands.

"You need to be careful," he said through his teeth. "You can't just go around saying what you want anymore. The world isn't like it used to be."

He turned his face up to stare at her desperately. His eyes shone in the dim lights of the dank room.

Zooey felt a sharp pang in her buttocks and shifted in her seat. Something about the look in his eyes told her to agree with him and promise anything he asked of her. "Okay, I won't say anything the rest of the time I'm here."

"I just want to make sure you come home and that you're all right." His melodic voice dripped with sincerity.

"I know. I want to come home too."

"Only six more days."

She gave a sad smile that pulled pathetically at the corners of her scabbed lips.

"And I'll be right out there waiting for you the minute you're released," he said.

"Two minutes!" the security officer bellowed.

Zooey leaned into the glass and touched her fingers to it, wishing she could feel the warmth of her friend. "Can't wait."

Chapter Twelve

The last week in the Undead Ward went by without incident. No one else was dragged through the doors, none of the other nurses were injured on the job, the food never got better, and Doctor Fullerton never gave up on asking if Zooey remembered anything from being a zombie. Finally, release day had arrived.

The Ward was in a frenzy that morning. The Undead were wired as they moved from room to room preparing for their release back into the world. Zooey stuck by her roommate as they went into the common area to pick out some clothes donated by the good people of Boston. She rummaged through the rags on the table and settled on a pair of brown dress shorts, an oversized burgundy tanktop, an old man style beige windbreaker, striped socks, and a pair of brown leather boots that were a size too big.

"I can't wait to get back home to my own clothes," she said under her breath to Chastity.

The girl broke down into tears, a lacy black bra clutched in her hands. She wiped her face with it and threw it back into the pile.

"What's wrong?" Zooey asked as she put a hand to her shoulder.

"Everyone is excited to go home to their families, or to get back to some life they left behind."

"Well, of course. Aren't you?"

The girl sobbed harder now. Zooey pulled her in for a hug. Her body was boney and cold.

"My family said they don't want me anymore. They're not coming to Boston and I can't leave. I have nothing to look forward to."

Zooey didn't like where this was going. "You have to have faith," she said. "The door is wide open, the slate's been wiped clean. Whoever we were before, we can be anyone we want now."

Chastity looked up from Zooey's chest where her head lay as tears ran down her scarred and freckled cheeks. "You really think so?"

"Oh yeah," she lied. "It's exciting!"

The girl took a step back and wiped at her face with her sleeve of her robe. "But I don't even know where I'm going to go once we're released. I have nowhere to stay."

Zooey looked around the room to see if anyone else was listening to the conversation and feeling charitable. Tamara Knox stood at the other end of the table, picking through the pile in search of anything with animal print. She pretended not to hear what the two girls were talking about.

Zooey sighed. "I guess you could stay with me, just until we found you something more permanent."

Chastity's face lit up. "Really?! That would be great! Thank you so much, Zooey! Thank you, thank you, thank you!" She hugged her roommate around the waist like a child would her mother.

Tamara finally looked over and tried her best to stifle a giggle. Zooey shot her a hateful glare and then looked up at the ceiling in exhaustion.

"How about we get changed and get the hell out of here," she said as she pried the girl's arms from her.

The group was led down through the hall and out through a different set of double doors to the main entryway. It was a pitiful sight of jumbled metal chairs and a front office protected by glass. Anyone coming in for the first time would think they had walked into a correctional facility and not a hospital.

"Your friends and family will be waiting for you out in the parking lot. For those of you who do not have anyone coming, there will be a city bus waiting to take you downtown and from there you're on your own," Nurse Shawn said robotically as he read from his clipboard.

Zooey looked on at the muscular nurse whose baby blue eyes matched his scrubs, and wondered if she'd come to miss his disinterested tone. She laughed under her breath. No chance!

"Here are your meal vouchers. It has a month's worth of coupons to get you free meals at various restaurants around town. We've also included three hundred dollars." He held up the cash and waved it around like he was at a strip club. "Use it wisely because once it runs out we will not be handing out any more. Secure a place to stay and find a job. Inside you will also find a pocket calendar with your Z-shot schedules already written in from now until the end of the year. Do not lose it and don't make us come looking for you."

Zooey's eyes searched the room as the nurse spoke. She wasn't sure what she was looking for, but her heart raced and her hands started to sweat. It wasn't until she'd scanned the faces of every Undead in the room and her eyes fell with disappointment that she realized she was looking for Ren.

"Good luck," Nurse Shawn said. "Now get out of here."

Two unfamiliar security officers opened the front doors, letting a blast of warm summer air into the room. Sunlight shone brightly in the blue sky. Birds sang from the branches of a nearby tree. Zooey shielded her eyes as she took a step outside. She inhaled a deep breath and felt the warmth of fresh air filtering out the stale hospital air that had built up in her chest.

Elizabeth and Oliver ran up to her with toothy smiles on their faces. Immediately, she was drawn in by hugging arms. Her body sank willingly into them.

"I'm so glad you're back," Elizabeth sighed into Zooey's hair.

"Me too."

They took a step away from each other and Elizabeth eyed the red-haired girl standing meekly behind her friend. "Who's this?"

"Oh right," Zooey said, almost forgetting the promise she'd made a few hours ago. "This is Chastity. She was my roommate and—well—um—she's coming to stay with us."

Elizabeth's eyes widened to orbs.

"But it's only for a little while," Zooey said quickly. "Till we can find her somewhere else and that won't even be that long because I didn't know they were going to give us cash upon release."

"You get paid to be a zombie?" Oliver said with a smile. "So unfair. I want to be Undead."

Zooey punched him in the arm and he faked massive pain with a howl.

"After walking through the mob in the parking lot you won't be singing that tune," Elizabeth said, straightening her blazer.

"Mob? What mob?" Zooey asked.

Chastity stood quietly in the background as if she didn't exist. When the group started forward, she followed like a ghost.

"A group of protesters decided to camp out in the lot," Elizabeth sneered. "But don't worry. We've got you."

Zooey's eyes narrowed as they rounded the corner. So a few people didn't think the Undead should be released back into society? It couldn't be any worse than Planned Parenthood dealt with every day.

But as the parking lot came into view, Zooey stopped, her mouth agape.

There were at least two hundred people holding signs that said things like "Go back to Hell, Monsters!" and "The dead should stay dead!" The dull roar of the crowd grew as they walked closer. It was nothing like the moans and groans of the horde of zombies she used to travel with, but she was sure these people were just as relentless.

Elizabeth threw her arm around Zooey's shoulder and led her forward. Oliver did the same for Chastity as the poor girl, who looked more virgin than monster in her long-sleeved floral dress, broke out into tears.

"Murderer!" several people screamed as they worked their way through the crowd to get to the car. "Kill yourself!"

Each word was like a punch in the gut. Zooey kept her eyes forward and tried not to let them fill with tears. It wouldn't help the situation. These people would never see her as a human being ever again. All she was to them was a grotesque walking dead woman.

Something hard hit her in the side of the head. She doubled over and pressed her hands to her right temple.

"Who threw that!?" Elizabeth screamed with all her might, the vein in the side of her forehead throbbing. She picked up a red apple from the ground and threw it as hard as she could back into the crowd. "Idiots! You're the ones who should go to Hell!"

Zooey felt a large hand on her back. She waited for it to shove her over as she clutched her beating head. It was Oliver. He cradled her to his heaving chest as he ushered both girls into the back of his van. He shut the doors without a word and hopped into the driver's seat. Something about that moment sent a wildfire of panic through Zooey. It was all too familiar, being locked away in a dark van. Outside, she could still hear Elizabeth shouting at the people outside with no signs of letting up.

"They're in, psycho! Let's get out of here," Oliver yelled with his colorful arm hanging out the window.

Zooey sat down on a guitar amp and lowered her head into her hands. She couldn't keep the tears in any longer. They streamed down her face and landed in a pool on the hard floor. She took deep breaths in through her nose and exhaled slowly through her mouth. It did little to stop the oncoming panic attack.

As the tires squealed, Zooey went flying into the side. Her body smashed into the paneling with a thud. Life on the outside was not off to a good start.

Chapter Thirteen

Zooey walked up the stairs to her old apartment above a restaurant in the Little Italy side of Boston. When she opened the front door she let out a drawn-out sigh. She was home. Chastity, Elizabeth, and Oliver followed closely behind, watching her like a zoo animal who had just been released back into the jungle. She flung her hospital goody-bag onto the small wooden table in the kitchen and flopped down on their second-hand couch.

"Your mother's worried about you. I said you'd call when you got home," Elizabeth's voice broke through the welcomed silence.

Zooey huffed and pushed herself up again. "Guess I'll get that over with now. Chastity, make yourself comfortable on the couch for the night. I think I'll just go to bed after I talk to them. I'm exhausted."

"Yeah, sure, of course," Elizabeth answered for everyone.

She turned and shoved Oliver out through the door with a pat on the back.

"I'll see you tomorrow, Zoe, we'll go for coffee or something if you're up for—" he hollered over his shoulder, but the door slammed in his face.

Zooey wanted to tell Elizabeth she was being rude, but she didn't have the energy. She shuffled to her room where she found her cellphone charging on her nightstand. She picked it up, sat down on the bed, and dialed home in Walker's Landing, Washington.

It rang six times before anyone answered.

"Bout time you called," a young man's voice said cheerfully.

"Yeah, I was a little busy dying and being brought back to life, Garrison. Where's mom? And why are you there? I thought you moved to L.A. or something?"

"Didn't work out. I'm just staying with the parentals until I can find another job."

Zooey rolled her eyes and sighed. "Sounds about right. Can I talk to mom?"

"Nice to talk to you too," her younger brother said bitterly. "MA! ZOOEY WANTS TO TALK TO YOU!"

She heard footsteps running into the room and then static as the phone was wrangled from her brother's hands. The two argued back and forth and then her mother wailed through the phone, "My girl, are you okay?! How could this have happened? I can't believe you were…I can't even…Oh, my poor girl!"

It was all too much for Zooey. She laid the phone in her lap and stared up at the ceiling. Now, all the sudden, she was her mother's little girl. What about when she was leaving for school and her mother couldn't be bothered to see her off at the airport because she had to visit Garrison in rehab again? When she put the phone back to her ear, her mother was still carrying on.

"What did they do to you in that hospital? Did they—"

"Mom!" Zooey said over her. "I'm fine. Everything's fine. I'm home now. I just wanted to let you know that everything is okay and I'm alive."

Her mother cried incoherently into the phone for a good ten minutes before Zooey made up an excuse to hang up.

"I have to take a shower, wash the day off. I'll call you later, okay?"

She hung up before her mother had a chance to argue and threw the phone onto the bed. Zooey knew her concern wasn't real, but a desperate attempt to fill a void from her brother's lack of drug abuse. Every so often he would go to rehab, get cleaned up, go job hunting, and act right for five minutes. For most families, this would be a joyous occasion. For Zooey's, though, it seemed to throw everything off balance.

Her mother spent every waking moment worrying about Garrison and doing everything she could to help him. When he wasn't in need of helping, she would turn her focus to her daughter, whom she usually ignored. These moments were never welcomed by Zooey, who spent most her childhood feeling neglected. She was a good kid who did her homework and never got into trouble, and for that she felt she'd been punished. No one in her family saw her. But now that she was an Undead, she could tell her mother was already trying to turn her into the new family project to escape the hatred she harbored for her husband. There was no way Zooey was going to let that happen.

She threw open the window and thrust her head out into the thick summer night air. The familiar sounds of her neighborhood came rushing at her—an old woman shouting out her window to her kids on the street, the hum of the people dining in the restaurant below, Oliver strumming his guitar and singing a song Zooey had never heard before.

She grabbed the straightened wire hanger by her bedside and tapped on the closed window next to hers. The music stopped and it slid open. Oliver stuck his orange head out with a wide grin.

"Took you long enough."

"It's been fifteen minutes."

"That's what I said."

She smiled and then bit her lip.

"What is it?" he asked with his head cocked.

He thrust the window up as far as it would go and sat down on the sill, leaning outward dangerously as he held onto the wall next to him. Zooey hated when he did this. She always pictured him falling to his death with a splat. He always argued he wouldn't die, just break his arms and legs. Now, though, she felt nostalgic as he leaned further back so his arms were outstretched. He was a kid who refused to grow up.

"It's just so weird…being back," Zooey said, the smile falling from her face. "It doesn't feel like home anymore. Not after what I did."

"Do you remember…what you did while you were out there?"

There was that question again. She was sure it wasn't the last time she'd hear it either. It would haunt her for the rest of her life. Unsure what to say, she shrugged her shoulders.

"Well, if you ever want to talk you know where to find me," he said casually, as if he weren't desperate to know her deepest secrets. "Elizabeth says you two are going shopping for school stuff tomorrow and to turn in your papers for registration."

"Well, if she said it then it must be true."

Whenever Oliver laughed it sounded like a song all in its own. He threw his head back and let it carry on the wind, drowning out the nearby woman's broken English. It carried on the breeze and echoed into the streets until it dissipated into silence. He looked at Zooey as if he were studying her.

"Zoe, are you sure you're okay?" It seems like something is really eating away at you."

She let out a small laugh, thinking he was making another zombie joke, but his face was stone-solid, his eyes filled with worry. She needed to say something, anything, to put his mind at ease. He could never know of the things she'd done. She couldn't bear it if he ever looked at her differently. Each time her eyes met his she worried she would catch a glimpse of fear.

"It's…" her brain scrambled to find the right words. "It's an Undead thing," she said finally.

Dammit. She promised herself she'd never use that phrase, but there it was.

"All right," he said. "Well, the offer stands…always."

She smiled softly and nodded. Oliver disappeared back into his room and he shut the window. Zooey left hers open and sat down on the edge of her bed. She pulled the cord to her bedside lamp and let the darkness encase her. Tomorrow was the real start to her Undead life. She groaned and threw herself back.

Ren's face flashed across her mind. She wished he was still around, that she could talk to him about everything that worried her. It was true what the hospital said. Things were different and the people who were closest to her wouldn't understand.

Being a zombie was easy. All she did was walk around, trip a few passers-by, eat their brains, and move on. Being brought back to life was the hard part. Everyone expected her to be the same person, but she wasn't. Nothing was the same and never would be.

A groaning voice came rushing up from the depths of her mind.

Brains.

"Oh no," she said aloud. "Not this again."

She closed her eyes and figured out how many more hours she had to get through until her next Z-shot—161. It was going to be a long week.

PLEASE LEAVE A REVIEW
ON AMAZON AND
GOODREADS!

THANK YOU!

And sign up for Alex Apostol's
mailing list for new releases,
giveaways, and more
(Get a free eBook!)
authoralexapostol.com

Made in the USA
Middletown, DE
26 November 2018